NOT MY LEGS!

Penelope S. Hession

Not My Legs!
Copyright © 2006

Penelope S. Hession

Cover design: Penelope Hession

ISBN: 978-0-6152-0416-1

This book
is dedicated to Jesus Christ
my healer,
who miraculously restored my eyesight
when I was going blind.

Other books:
Cast Your Nets
Wipe My Tears*
Jeep
Two Nights of Courage
Grunt, Brute, and The Lady

The author can be reached at:
sdssolutions@msn.com

*Father Jon series
This is the second book in the Father Jon series.

As she rounded the curve, the headlights coming straight at her blinded Jessie. She screamed as she struggled to make her car invisible to the oncoming monster. "Jesus!"

The eerie silence that followed the head-on collision was deafening. Dust, steam and smoke mingled in the aftermath. Jessie opened her eyes. The windshield was gone, and so was the front of her car. It appeared that the other car was sitting where her motor used to be. She tried to move and caught her breath as pain raged up her spine. Her legs were trapped under or in something. Amazingly, her head and face were without blemish. A rear view mirror, hers she thought, hung right in front of her. The steering wheel pinned her right arm to the seat.

No sound issued from the attacking monster. The only sound she could hear was the sizzling steam from the radiators.

"Oh, my God," a voice exclaimed somewhere beyond the dust.

"Use the cell phone, call 911!" another voice cried out.

"Do you suppose anyone is alive?"

Jessie tried to cry out, but just the inhaling hurt so much. She moaned instead.

"Sounds like someone is!"

"They are on their way."

"Good."

"Don't get too close, the cars might explode!"

"There is someone in there, I can see her."

"Wait for the paramedics. They'll be here soon. I can hear their sirens."

"That might be too late for whoever she is!" The speaker had climbed over the torn guardrail and was leaning into the car. "Hi, help is on the way." Jessie nodded.

"Can you move any?"

"Only my head, mouth, eyelids. My arm is trapped, and I don't know where the other one is." Jessie managed a weak smile.

"Do you know Jesus?"

"Yes, He is my best friend."

"Great. What is your name?"

"Jessie."

"Lord, Jessie needs you help right now. She is hurting and trapped. Send her ministering angels. Thank you Lord, Jesus. Amen."

Jessie closed her eyes during the prayer.

"Are you still there?"

"Yes," She whispered.

The oncoming sirens stopped. "Thank God!" the man said as he stepped back to let the professionals get to the cars.

Twenty minutes after the crash, the paramedics began to assess the victims. Jessie was the only one alive. "Well, honey, we will have to get you untangled from this mess." A young paramedic climbed into the remains of the car with her. Your name is Jessie? Right?"

2

Jessie responded with a slight sound.

A blood pressure cuff was worked around her pinned arm. The paramedic was checking her temperature and heartbeat rate.

"Where is my other arm?" she finally managed to squeak out.

The medic ran gentle hands across her shoulder and found her arm wedged in an unnatural position. "Right here. Broken but attached." He smiled. His breath smelled like spearmint gum. "It is you legs in the car engine that are a problem."

Jessie grimaced as something put more pressure on her lower limbs. "That hurts!"

"I'm surprised she can feel anything." Another medic struggled to keep his balance at the edge of her car.

Jessie closed her eyes, hoping that when she opened them again, all of this would be just a bad dream. She listened to the talking between the medics. Suddenly, she opened her eyes. "Did you say you would have to cut off my legs? No, I will not give you permission to do that. Get them out of the engine whole."

"It's OK, Jessie, we are just discussing options. Your legs will never be the same. Honey, we need to consider all the factors pertaining to you life, not just your legs."

Jessie screamed. "My legs are part of my life!"

Spearmint gum spoke up. "Hey guys, you are making the situation worse. Can't you do your talking elsewhere?"

Jessie cried out again. "No permission to cut my legs off!" She seemed to loose consciousness.

"You heard her," the paramedic was speaking into the radiophone.

"We have the 'jaws of life' heading out right now. Let's see what they can do."

Spearmint gum grumbled. "You really pushed her blood pressure up. Wonder how much blood she is loosing. Pass me a plasma bag."

Jessie felt the prick and opened her eyes. Spearmint inserted a needle and readied the plasma bag. "You're watching," he said.

Jessie mouthed 'yes'.

"This is just in case we need this." The sounds of a heavy truck came closer. "Jaws of life," he said.

For over an hour, men worked to first peel the other car's engine away from her and then to remove bit by bit the engine casing that encased her legs and feet. Spearmint touched her often and kept up a quiet line of chat to help her. Occasionally, when the workers moved her even a tiny bit, she would moan. When she said anything, it was in monosyllables. Spearmint learned she trusted in God, and she was determined not to lose her legs. He admired her strength.

Finally, they had her legs free and wrapped in sterile coverings. "We are going to try to move you now."

The steering wheel had been removed, and her right arm was miraculously only bruised, not broken. A new IV had been inserted. Spearmint leaned over her and looked her straight in the eyes. "I need to put you under so that we can move you without you feeling so much pain. I give you my word, yours legs are still there, and you won't be under very long."

Jessie tried to say 'no', but he just shook his head. "Trust me."

Now she lay on a gurney in the emergency

room of some hospital. A nurse was taking her vitals and mumbling about stubborn patients. Jessie thought a moment before she said, "If it was your legs…"

The nurse just pursed her lips and kept on writing on the chart.

Jessie prayed. After all, what else could she do, she thought. Later, she would marvel that she was so lucid at that point to be able to think. A doctor came up and looked at the mess that was her legs. He shook his head as he walked away.

"Honey, we are waiting on the surgeon and an operating room."

"My name is Jessie."

"They saved your legs out there, but I'm not so sure they'll . . ."

Jessie interrupted. "Do not cut off my legs! God will heal them. He is in the healing business."

"Don't get smart with me, young lady!"
Jessie wanted to cry out but instead began to pray again. The nurse watched her lips move and thought Jessie was probably cursing her. "That attitude won't do you any good."

Someone came up. Jessie looked to see who it was. It was a priest. He seemed to be using a cane. He leaned over her and asked if she would like him to pray with her. Jessie nodded. He pulled out a small bottle of oil to anoint her and prayed. When he finished, he touched her less injured hand. "Is there anything else I can do, anyone to call?"

"I need an advocate."

"What?"

"I need an advocate."

"Don't you have family that can come."

"No," Jessie whispered. "I need someone to stand up for me so that they don't cut off my legs."

"Are they going to do that?"

"They say they won't, but when I am unconscious, what will they do then? I need an advocate to say no."

It took the priest only a split moment to consider her request. "Do you want me to be that advocate?"

"Yes, please."

"We had better put this in writing." Jon was having mixed emotions.

She nodded. Jon quickly obtained a pad of paper and wrote out what Jessie dictated. It was straightforward and simple. She had him hold her less injured hand so she could scribble her name on the paper. The priest signed it, and a passing orderly witnessed both signatures.

He copied it at the copy machine and placed a copy under her head as they came to move her to the operating room. "Who is the surgeon?" the priest asked.

"Forbes."

Jon smiled. This was the same surgeon who did the work on him. "Good. Tell him to read the paper. I'll be in the Family Waiting Room if he has a question."

"Father, you can go in to the upper operating room theater watch and wait there. You are a Chaplain. That is one of your privileges."

Father Jon Mark nodded and followed the gurney to the inner door. As they stopped to open the door, he looked down into Jessie's face and remembered another young lady who died in his arms. "God is with you. I will be waiting for you." Jessie looked at him and smiled ever so slightly as they pushed her on into the operating room.

Father Jon took the restricted elevator to the next level and went into the observation galley above the operating room. Two interns were studying in the

6

front row. "Can I sit here?" Jon asked.

They nodded. One said, "Dr. Forbes is in the operating room. This should be a good surgery."

Jon nodded back and settled his cane at his feet. He could see Jonathan Forbes reading the paper attached to the head of the gurney. The doctor looked up and waved to Father Jon. He switched on the operating room PA. "I'll do my best. How are you doing, Father?"

One of the interns toggled the talk switch. "Very well, thank you. That young lady is determined to keep her legs."

"So I have been told. This will probably be a long surgery." Jonathan pulled his facemask over his mouth and turned to speak to the anesthetist about something.

Jon watched the preliminary opening of the bandages before leaving the galley. He made his way to the Chapel and sat before the shrine of St. Elizabeth of Hungary to pray. For hours he stayed, petitioning the Lord for a miracle for a young lady named Jessie. He thought of all the hours he had spent praying for others in the past. He regretted that he could not stretch out prone to pray. That had always been a special place for him. His leg was healing, but they told him it would be two years before the muscles and torn tissues had regenerated and developed much strength.

The police sharp shooter whose bullet had shattered his leg after passing through the intended person was still distraught about Father's injury. He had been to see Jon several times since Vincent Sardoni was killed after Vincent took aim at Father Jon. Father appreciated that he was alive and had prayed with the policeman several times that his remorse at Father's injury be relieved.

"Father, can you pray with me?" a quiet

voice spoke. Jon looked and saw a young man, bravely holding back his tears.

"Of course," Jon answered.

The young man bent double in grief and sobbed. "My wife just died."

Jon moved in close to the young man. "Father," he beseeched God, "We need you right here, right now."

He held the sobbing young man for some time. When the young man's crying subsided a little, he began talking about his wife and her death. She was nineteen and had taken an overdose. The young man claimed he did not know his wife was doing drugs. Jon doubted that but said nothing.

"I suppose you think I am a drug pusher or addict or something, too?" The young man turned angrily on Father Jon.

Jon shook his head. "No."

"Her parents think I gave her the drugs!"

"Did you?"

The young man stiffened. "No!"

Jon continued to hold the young man as he prayed for wisdom. "Do you know who did?" He asked the question quietly.

The young man nodded. "Her sister."

"Do her parents know that?"

"No," he whimpered. "What do I tell the police? I ran out of the room when they confirmed she was dead. They will be looking for me."

"Do they know your name?"

"Of course!"

"Then I suppose you will have to talk with them pretty soon."

The young man sniffed and nodded. "But what do I tell them?"

"The truth."

"They'll never believe me. And her parents

will tell them I am lying."

"Are you?"

The young man jerked violently from Father Jon's grasp, causing Jon's cane to go skidding across the floor.

"You're no help!" screamed the young man as he shoved Father aside and ducked out of the chapel.

Jon knelt on the floor and prayed before he retrieved his cane and attempted to stand. It wasn't easy to get up any more. He reached over and pulled the 'panic cord' on the wall. Within minutes, an orderly was helping him to his feet.

"I thought they told you not to try to kneel for awhile yet," the orderly teased. "Did ya forget?" Jon smiled, "Sometimes the knees are where the Lord wants us. Only thing is, I can't get up by myself yet."

In the surgery theater, Dr. Forbes was explaining to the watching interns about the new, state of the art technique he was using on his patient. "You remember, Father Jon was the first we tried it on here. As this surgery began, Father was up in the galley with some of you. This young lady is fortunate to be healthy and determined to save her legs. Now we will see how the healing goes. The several young men and women in the galley applauded the doctor as he left the operating theater.

Feeling a little stiff from his time kneeling and the violent shove that had put him on the floor, Jon navigated his way back to the surgery area and recovery rooms.

Dr. Forbes was coming out of a recovery room. "They are back together, her legs. There will be considerable restorative surgery needed to get the damaged tissue replaced." He smiled at Father Jon. "What ever made you agree to be her advocate to keep us from amputating them?"

"She caught me in the hall and asked."

"Do you think she was in her right mind?"

"I didn't make a judgment," Jon answered. "I just responded. Of course, it helped that you saved my leg several months ago."

Doctor Forbes nodded. "I hope we did the right thing for her."

"You did," Chaplain Jon Mark said as he patted the doctor on the shoulder, "you did."

Downstairs, security detained the young man whose wife had died. He pouted, called them pigs, and in general behaved poorly. "What right do you have to detain me?" he screamed.

"Where did you go in such a rush when they told you that your wife was dead of an overdose?" The security officer was used to drunks and drug addicts in the emergency room.

"To the chapel to pray!"

"Did anybody see you go there?"

"There was a crippled priest there."

"Oh, Father Jon. Did you talk to him?"

"Yeah, but I didn't tell him nothing."

The security officer picked up the phone and dialed intercom. "Father Jon, Security; Father Jon, Security."

Dr. Forbes looked at Jon. "It sounds like you are a wanted man."

Chaplain Jon Mark nodded. "Probably about the hot head I met in the Chapel."

"You are never bored here, are you?"

Jon laughed, "No."

"Father Jon, Security. Father Jon, Security" sounded the intercom again.

"See you later," Jon waved good-bye to the doctor and took the first elevator going down to ground level.

10

In an adjoining room in security, the distraught parents of the recently deceased young woman were answering questions with another security officer. "We have no idea how she got the drugs!" The father stated over and over again. "It was probably that boy she was hanging around. Something like this has never happened in our family."

The security officer wrote down their statements. "Even her sister doesn't know! Why are you questioning us? Can't you see that we have just lost a daughter, and it is quite a shock to her mother and me?"

"Yes, I understand," the security officer spoke with a calm voice. "It is just procedure, especially when we are acutely aware that an overdose was taken." What he didn't say was the particular overdose had been laced with a poison. "And we will ask that 'boy'. Thank you for your time and help. Do you need help getting home?"

"We drove ourselves. That boy rode with us. We never want to see him again!" As the dead girl's parents left the security area, they could hear 'that boy' screaming and ranting in another office. Because they were not looking where they were going as they listened to the boy's remarks, they physically ran into a hospital chaplain.

"Sorry," Father Jon murmured.

"Oh Chaplain, Chaplain Jon Mark," the father was reading Jon's nametag. "We just lost our daughter. Is it normal procedure to be pulled into the Security rooms and asked questions about our daughter's life?"

"I have no idea," Jon answered, wondering if this was the nineteen year old who overdosed. "I am sorry you lost your daughter. Would you like me to pray with you?"

11

"No, that won't be necessary," the woman responded stiffly. "We have our own pastor." Jon nodded and continued on into the Security Offices. He could hear the young man swearing and cursing. He tapped lightly on the door.

"Come in," a voiced yelled.

As Jon entered, the young man made a dive for the open door. Jon reached out his cane and tripped him.

"You have no right . . .!" the young man yelled.

Jon smiled. "Seems you knocked me down upstairs. I was only trying to help you."

Another security officer had entered the room at that moment and assisted the young man back to a chair.

"So you know him?" asked the first security officer.

"I was praying in the Chapel when he asked me if I could help him. So I prayed with him."

"Did he tell you anything unusual or try to get you to take something for him?"

"I just treated him as I would any other distraught person in this hospital. Although, I must say he did leave me rather suddenly."

The hostility in the young man's face softened for a moment.

"He knocked you down?"

"Let's say I was shoved aside rather violently."

The police officer looked at the young man. "Shoving a Chaplain, hmm, could throw the book at you."

The officer picked up the phone and dialed the city police. "Have you gotten the report yet?" he asked someone at the other end. "Oh really. OK, we will. Thanks."

12

"What is that all about?" blurted out the young man.

Before the security officer could answer, there was a knock on the door, and two city patrolmen entered. The young man blanched. "James Roger Crouse?"

The security officer nodded. They snapped handcuffs on the young man and led him out of the room.

"That is a little harsh isn't it for a man whose wife just died." Jon stated.

"She wasn't married to him, and . . ."

Jon put up his hand, "OK, don't say any more."

"Did he really knock you down? Was it on purpose?"

"Yes and yes."

"Seems like we see more and more people like that kid. Wonder what the world is coming to." The security officer closed the folder he had in front of him.

Jon thought about the young men at St. Ignatius and smiled. "Some are growing up to be law abiding adults."

"Thanks for coming down. By the way, the Chapel will be closed for a while." Jon raised an eyebrow. "That young man left a 'stash' in there. Cleaning personnel found it."

Jon skipped lunch while he was in the Chapel, so he opted for dinner in the cafeteria. Balancing his tray with one hand, using his cane with the other, an intern came up and took the tray. "Here, sit with us. We saw you up there watching Dr. Forbes. Tell us what it looks like to a non-medic."

Jon sat down as six or seven interns pulled their chairs in closer to him. "Well, since I am walking proof of the good doctor's talents, what do you want to know?"

A couple of them grinned. "I remember the argument about whether or not to try to save your leg. It was the first time I was assisting in the surgery. Dr. Forbes said he didn't think it was fair to keep you from genuflecting for the rest of your life." There were giggles around the table.

"What is genuflecting?" someone asked.

"That is when I kneel with one knee before the altar or when I come into church. It is helpful to have two legs."

"I can't imagine that with only one leg." An intern stood up and tried to kneel, pretending he had only one leg. They all laughed at him as they helped him up off the floor.

"Why is this patient so emphatic about keeping her legs?

"I don't know," Jon answered. "I am just the advocate."

"You ought to hear the talk going around about that."

"Sssssss."

Then someone acted out one of the resident doctors who is very opinionated. "Iffff that Chaplaaaaaain is going to interfeeeeer with oooouuurrrr surgery, theeeeen heeeeee neeeeeds to geeeeet a doooctoooors liiiicense. Yeeees siiiir, heeee jjjjjust thiiiiinks heeees GOD!" Those around the table erupted in more laughter.

Jon looked down for a moment before quietly stating. "It does help to have a first hand relationship with God." The interns got quiet. "I guess that is my role. I don't think I am God, but I do know Him, and He knows me."

Most had finished eating by then and excused themselves to go study or go back on duty. One lingered after the others. "Father, can we talk sometime, like not here, but in private?"

"Yes, call and make an appointment when you are available. I'll meet you either in the Chapel or in that set of tiny rooms they call my apartment."

"Thanks, Father."

In recovery, Jon found Jessie awake but heavily sedated. She tried to talk but the words came out all slurred and thick. Father Jon assured her that she still had her legs. A faint smile crossed her face. "It will be a long recovery," Jon said. "My leg and muscles will not be fully recovered for about eighteen more months."

Jessie nodded.

Jon turned to the nurse. "When will she be moved to a room?"

"Dr. Forbes wants to wait until in the morning. He is keeping an eagle eye on the wound for infection."

Father Jon nodded and took Jessie's less injured hand in his. "Father God, we know that you have seen to the repair of Jessie's legs. Father, we now ask for you to keep all infection away and give her a quick and complete healing. And, for tonight, that Jessie can rest and be assured that you are with her." Jon gave her hand a little squeeze. She tightened one finger around his.

He made the sign of the cross with oil on her forehead. She nodded slightly. "Good night Jessie. If you need me, have the nurse phone me. I live here in the hospital." Again she nodded.

As Jon walked with his limp and cane down the halls, he thought of all the others who had been in his life for a season. He marveled that God could so quickly place them in his path. While he was considering this thought, a voice, a sweet and gentle voice, was calling. "Father Jon, Father Jon."

When he stopped and turned, he saw the

diminutive Sister Margaret Louise hurrying after him as fast as she could push her new walker. The elderly sister had had both hips replaced and needed the walker for stability and balance.

"My dear Sister Margaret Louise, don't fret, I will wait for you."

"Good," she chirped. She was out of breath when she arrived at Father's side.

"Do you have time to talk?" she asked.

"For you, I always have time." They were in front of a small patient lounge. "Do you want to sit in one of the chairs?"

"No, there is too much sitting already," and she smiled. "Let us go out on the patio."

"Isn't it a little cool tonight?"

"You have Jesus, don't you?" she replied. "And I've got my sweater."

Jon laughed and opened the door to the patio. It wasn't too cold. Spring was in the air, and this patio, sheltered from the winds by large panels of translucent plastic, kept it useable almost all year round.

Sister Margaret Louise looked out over the city and smiled. "It is going to be a good spring." Father Jon nodded and knew that she was more interested in something else than just checking on the weather.

"When are you going to be able to go back to the convent?"

"That's what I want to speak to you about. I don't want to seem presumptuous, but they do seem to be slow about letting me go."

Jon smiled at her. She had visited him after his surgery, and often they said the Rosary together while he was still bedridden. She had been a big encouragement whenever she came to his hospital room, pushing that walker before her. "It would

16

seem to me that you have much to do while you are still in the hospital."

"Just because I am as old as Methusalah, I don't have to be sheltered all the time."

"And just how old is that?" Father Jon asked. With a twinkle in her eyes, she replied. "Old enough to be your great, great grandmother."

"Now, that is old." Jon smiled.

"But, I feel like they have put me out to pasture, leaving me here." She blushed. "Oh my, I shouldn't have said that. My vows of obedience."

"Your secret is safe with me, Sister Margaret Louise. What can I do to help you feel better about staying here?"

The sister was staring out at the stars. "Forgive me for bothering you, Father. Please hear my confession."

Father Jon nodded and waited as Sister Margaret Louise confessed her shortcomings, including her attitude toward the hospital stay.

"I really don't know what has gotten into me. I have never been rebellious or raised my voice about anything." She looked again, far off. Her voice broke. "They think I may have cancer too."

Slowly, Jon exhaled.

"I wanted to be in the convent, not here, when I meet my Lord. It is there where I dedicated my life and lived!"

Jon nodded. "Can I make a suggestion?"

Sister Margaret Louise nodded.

"Go visit a young lady by the name of Jessie in the morning, like you did for me. Both of her legs were badly hurt in a car accident today. Dr. Forbes is her doctor. She needs a great, great, great grandmother to encourage her now."

The petite nun nodded. "Thank you, Father." Jon held the door open as Sister Margaret Louise

17

pushed her walker ahead of her and reentered the hospital with firm steps.

Once in her room, Sister Margaret Louise knew she had to humble herself and pray for divine forgiveness. True, Father Jon had spoken the words, but she was the one who had sinned. She removed her outer garments and slowly lowered herself to the floor. She lay with her face on the hard surface and began to pray. She knew she must stay there until the Lord released her.

The night nurse came in and gasped. She started to reach for the 'call cord' when she realized that the sister was praying and had not fallen out of bed. "Sister, are you all right?"

"Yes," came the muffled reply.

"Don't you want to get up and pray on your bed?"

"No," again the muffled reply.

The nurse was in a quandary. If anyone else found her on the floor, they would report the nurse to be negligent in her duties. She wondered what she should do. She could keep the rest of the night shift out of the nun's room and, barring the doctor coming in before 6 A.M.; no one would bother the elderly nun. Still, she was worried. She detached the call cord from the bed and placed it by the sister's hand. "Call me if you need me."

Sister Margaret Louise touched the call cord with her hand. The nurse hoped that was an affirmation that the good nun would call her if she needed the nurse.

At the nursing station, the nurse confided in the other RN on duty. "She what?"

"Ssssssh."

"You left her there?"

"I don't think it would have done us any good to put her back in bed. She knows what she is

18

doing."

"And, what is that?"

"Praying."

The two nurses looked at each other. "We've never had this kind of problem before. Her doctor will have a cow and our jobs if he finds out."

"The evening shift said she was looking for Father Jon. Let's call him and see if he has any ideas."

The phone rang and Jon knew it was too soon to be a wake-up call. "Father Jon," he answered trying to make his voice sound normal. The clock said 11:15 P.M.

"I'm sorry to bother you, Father, but it's about Sister Margaret Louise."

"What is the matter with her?"

"Nothing that we can tell, only, Father, she is on her face on the floor praying."

Jon was sitting on the edge of the bed and had turned on a lamp.

"Praying?"

"Yes Father, she said she was alright and did not want to be gotten off the floor. We are concerned that she will get cold."

"And that her doctor will find out, right?" Jon instinctively knew the nurses were concerned for the patient and for themselves.

"Right."

"Will she let you cover her with a blanket?"

"I don't know, we didn't try."

"Don't put it under her, just on top. And tell her that Father Jon told you to do that. Then call me back."

There was no response on the phone. Jon heard the one nurse tell the other one what he had said before the line went dead.

He sat for a few moments with his hands

covering his face as he sought what God would want him to do. He remembered the look on her face when she had left him. It was a look of self-sorrow and determination to purge herself of her sin. He inhaled deeply and exhaled when he became aware of what he had to do.

The phone rang. Jon just answered with 'hello'.

"She accepted the blanket when we told her that you had said she should be covered with it. She seems alright, and her vital signs are normal."

"Call me if there is any change and call me before you two leave in the morning. I'll be praying for her during the night.'

"Thanks, Father." He heard the disconnection click.

He placed the phone on the floor and carefully rolled to the floor. Getting up in the morning might be tricky, but, for the night, he would intercede for Sister Margaret Louise while prone on the floor. He reached up and turned off the lamp.

At five in the morning, the phone rang again. Jon reached over to answer it, stiff from his night on the floor. "Father Jon"

"We just put her in bed. She has the most peaceful look on her face."

"Praise God, who is merciful in all His ways. Do you have an orderly up there right now."

"No, Father, they are all down in ER during the night unless we call for one. Do you need us to get you one?"

"No, I'll call down there if I need to. Thanks, and God bless you for letting her make her peace with God."

The nurse looked at the phone. "What did he say?" The other nurse looked concerned.

"He said, 'God bless you for letting her make

her peace with God'.'"

"I'm glad we did what we did."

"So am I."

It was a struggle, but no one could see the awkward positions that Father Jon tried before he finally got up on the bed. He rested there a short while before getting up. Then, Jon said to himself before he went to take a shower, "It's going to be a long day. Maybe I will take a nap this afternoon."

The physical therapist took Jon through the usual paces, trying to get Jon to walk with a smoother gait. He had Jon sit and stand, watching how the priest coped with regular chairs and then a soft couch. Jon practiced each suggested move a dozen times or so. Finally, the therapist had Jon recline on the bed they used in therapy. He stretched Jon's damaged leg; then folded it up until Jon thought the pain would never stop.

"Now, Father, let me see how you get up from this mattress."

"With or without my cane?" Jon asked.

"Can you do it without your cane?"

Jon nodded. He twisted himself to the edge of the bed, and by rolling sideways, managed to stand up unaided.

"Not bad. In a week or two, we ought to be able to have you getting up from the floor."

An impish grin crossed Jon's face. "I can do that, too."

"What? But I haven't worked on that with you. Have you fallen and had no one to get you up?"

"No, but I was pushed down, and an orderly did pick me up. However, last night, I was on the floor in my room in prayer and was able to get up this morning from the hard floor by myself?"

The physical therapist was noting

information in Jon's chart. "What did you say?"

"Do you want me to show you how I did it?"

"Did what?"

"Got up off the floor this morning."

The therapist looked at Jon, trying to figure out if Jon was pulling his leg. "OK, Father, show me."

"Actually, the hard part is getting down." Jon cautiously lowered himself to the floor, using the bed as a halfway point. He then rolled so his face was down at the floor. "This is where I started from."

In amazement, his physical therapist watched as Jon reversed the process of getting down to the floor and after several moments was standing again. "I hope you aren't doing that too often. Your doctor would have a fit."

"But it works doesn't it?" Jon asked grinning.

"Yeah, but the doctor doesn't want that kind of stress on that leg yet."

"In other words, call for help if I get down."

"Yep, no sense in overdoing it right yet." Jon tucked his loose shirt into the top of the sweatpants he wore for therapy. "Don't tell the doctor, and I won't do it again unless absolutely necessary. OK?"

The two men looked at each other smiling. "Personally, I think it is terrific, but I know Dr. Forbes wants to take it a little more slowly to insure you have no setbacks."

"OK, I can live with that," Jon answered. Tomorrow morning, same time?"

"Yes."

Jon moved slowly back towards his apartment. He needed to change into clerical garb before making rounds. He was always slow going

22

back after therapy. It was quite a workout under normal circumstances, and he had gotten up off the floor by himself two times already today.

He showered and put on his priestly clothes and then sank down on the bed for a nap. He had to admit to himself that getting up twice and the usual therapy, along with the long night of prayer, had sapped his strength. He set his alarm for two hours and immediately fell asleep.

He wondered how long the phone had been ringing when he finally woke. "Father Jon."

"Are you alright, Father," an anxious voice inquired.

"I think so."

"Sorry to bother you, but we have a situation in ER. Can you come down?"

"I'll be right there."

Jon got up, somewhat stiffly but rested, and picked up his stole, holy oil and a small leather case with communion elements. He took a quick look in the mirror and smoothed his hair into place before he went out the door with his cane.

In Emergency, there were several gurneys with people on them. "Over here, Father," he heard a voice call.

Pushing past nurses and orderlies and a doctor, Jon reached the gurney closest to the elevator. A pale-faced pregnant woman was on it. She was in labor, and the nurses seemed to be preparing her for delivery. "Auto accident. She has twins, she is about 30 weeks, and we are going for surgery as there seems to be a blockage." The woman moaned and grabbed for something to hang onto."

Jon reached for her hand as another contraction came right on the heels of the first one. He began praying and anointed her with oil. She barely was aware of him as another contraction was taking place.

The conversation around him was rapid and becoming frantic as the ER nurses monitored the woman's vital signs. A doctor kept saying, "Try to hold her off on delivery a few more minutes." The elevator door opened, and the whole group moved as one into the elevator. Jon's hand, clutched in a death-like grip by the woman, backed into the elevator before the gurney. He kept praying as the elevator rose rapidly to the 4th floor. The door opened on the opposite side. Jon was pushed ahead of the gurney as the nurses hurried the woman toward an operating room.

At the entrance to the operating theater, someone said to Jon, "You'll have to let her go now." He nodded but found it almost impossible to get his hand free. Someone pried the woman's fingers from his hand and rushed her on into the room. As the doors shut, he could hear the woman crying out. He sat on an examination stool and prayed. More personal rushed by him. Jon wanted so badly to go to her. Memories of past experiences raced through his thoughts.

In what seemed like an eternity of time, a staff member came out of the operating room. "Babies on way to preemie nursery. Both are breathing on their own."

"Mother?" Jon asked.

"Delivery wise, OK, but considerable internal injuries. Amazingly enough, babies were not affected by the airbag and seatbelt. She'll be in ICU when we get done."

Jon nodded. "What is her name?"

"Mary Linden."

Jon took the elevator that took him directly to the newborn, preemie and critical birth nurseries. A

24

nurse looked at him as he stepped out of the elevator. "Wash your hands and put on a gown." Jon complied. He had never visited this part of the hospital, but his identification badge gave him access. After donning the loose gown over his clothing, Jon headed towards the preemie nursery. "Put on a face mask!" This order came from a voice behind a face-mask. Jon picked up the gauze mask from the indicated plastic tub and pulled it over his face. He looked like all the others in the area except for his black pants and shoes showing below the gown.

"The twins just born down in surgery?" Jon asked as two sets of nurses working on the babies.

"Yes."

"I want to baptize them?"

"They are Catholic?"

"Mother is."

The nurse handed him a bottle of sterile water. "Use this."

Jon nodded as she moved him in close to the babies.

Moments later, Jon christened each child with the sterilized water as the nursing staff continued on with the preparation of the babies for the incubators. Baby A was a boy. Baby B was a girl. Jon removed the gown and mask as he left the nursery. He picked up an in-house phone and called back to the operating area. Mary Linden was still in surgery. He left word for them to page him when she was moved to ICU.

He checked on the room number for Jessie and found she was on floor three. He took the elevator, carefully favoring his weaker leg.

He spoke with a nurse about Jessie. He started to her room, only to be met in the hall by a rejoicing Sister Margaret Louise.

"Father, Father!" Sister Margaret Louise was

breathless.

"What is it Sister Margaret Louise?"

"That girl Jessie, she is so lovely. She believes God intervened when He sent you along as His angel."

"Whoa, I'm no angel." Father Jon laughed.
Sister Margaret Louise smiled. "Well, you were His messenger last night for me, and I guess you can be His angel for her."

"I'm glad to see you so happy and contented." Jon responded. "How is Jessie? I was just on the way to see her."

"Sort of drugged but so pleased that her legs are still intact." Sister Margaret Louise looked down at her own legs. "Just as I am pleased that I can still walk and get about. A nurse gave her a shot for pain while I was there. She may be sleeping now."

"That won't hurt my feelings," Jon replied. "I had a stressful therapy this morning and could use another nap."

Sister Margaret Louise patted him on the hand. "I don't suppose that will bother the sleeping Jessie." Sister started walking away from Father. "Oh, yes, Father," she said as she turned back to him. "If God wants me to remain here in the hospital, it is alright."

Jon looked at her, amused. "But, you would really like to be across the street?"

Sister nodded her head slightly.

"Keep praying, Sister."

Sister Margaret Louise pushed her walker before her and left Father Jon standing alone in the hall.

"Jessie is asleep," said the nurse he had talked with earlier.

Jon nodded. "I think I need a rest anyway. Will you call me when she wakes?"

26

"Certainly."

Jon walked with his cane more slowly than usual. His leg did not hurt, but his muscles were very sore and tired. He begged God's forgiveness for overstressing his injured body as he made his way to the East Wing and his apartment.

His phone was ringing when he entered. "Father Jon."

Father Marvin, the priest at St. Ignatius, greeted him. He was calling to see if Father Jon would like an evening out at the parish. The 'boys' would all be around as well as Ramon and Hilda.

"I don't drive yet."

"Ramon can pick you up. Let's say about 4 P.M.?"

Father Jon was elated to be asked to visit the St. Ignatius Parish. It was the parish he had been at when his leg was shattered. "There is a young lady I must see sometime later today. Can I call you a little later and confirm?"

"Must be an important young lady," Father Marvin said.

"Yes, she is the one that was in the auto accident yesterday morning, the one whose legs were trapped in the car motor."

"Were they able to save her legs?" Father Marvin asked.

"Yes, Dr. Forbes, you remember he was the one who operated on me, was the surgeon. So she and I have something in common." Jon chuckled. "Glued together leg bones."

"Before long there will be a whole group of you 'synthetic bone bonded people'." Father Marvin laughed. "Call me as soon as you can."

About two-thirty, a nurse phoned Father Jon for Jessie. "Father, I heard you came to see me, and I was asleep." Jessie mumbled into the phone

Jon struggled as he wakened from his second nap of the day. "How are you doing?"

"A lot of pain, but I am glad to have both legs. You sent that nun?"

"Sister Margaret Louise, yes. She came to see me after my surgery."

"I couldn't remember her name, Sister Margaret Louise. There, I had the nurse write it down. Is she really in her 80's?"

"That's what they tell me."

"When are you coming by? I want to have all my make-up on." Jessie grimaced in pain.

"When do you want me to come?" Jon asked.

"Tomorrow morning? I feel pretty awful now."

"I'll come after my therapy about eleven. Will that be OK?"

"Sure, here comes the nurse with the pain hypo. See you - bye."

Jon remember those first few days after his leg had been shattered by the ricocheting bullet that had passed through the terrorist who tried to kill him. The days had been pain filled and a blur after every pain-relieving hypodermic. He laid back in the therapeutic recliner and thought about going back to sleep. 'St. Ignatius!' he remembered suddenly.

A quick call confirmed that Ramon would pick him up at four-thirty.

Father Jon contacted St. Charles Rectory, the church in the next block from the hospital complex, telling them he would be out for the evening so they might get a page for a Catholic chaplain at the hospital. Jon then notified the offices of the hospital so that all his pages would be sent to St. Charles.

He pulled the packet of papers out from his desk that informed him about what his doctor wanted him to do in his recovery. In it was a paragraph about leaving the hospital grounds. He groaned. Dr. Forbes said that when he was outside of the hospital complex, he had to be in a wheelchair.

Jill, an assistant in Therapy, answered the phone. "I have a problem." Jon stated. "I am going outside of the hospital complex for the evening, and Dr. Forbes states on my treatment papers that I must go in a wheelchair."

"Just a minute, Father, I'll see if Tony is still here." There was a clatter as the telephone fell from wherever Jill had placed it. In a few minutes, she returned. "He has already left. Sorry about the phone dropping off the desk. It would seem that if that is what Dr. Forbes wrote, then you had better follow it."

Jon laughed. "I was afraid of that. But, you see, I have a problem. I don't have a wheelchair."

There was a brief silence on the other end before Jill spoke up. "We do not have any more scheduled for therapy this afternoon. I suppose we could loan you one if you promise to have it back before seven in the morning."

"That won't get you into any kind of trouble, will it?"

"No, Father, we have had to loan out a chair every so often when an in-house patient was permitted to go somewhere on leave. And besides, there are at least a hundred wheelchairs sitting around in the hospital unused during the nights. Only in a major disaster would a request come for ours."

"Like the fires and bombings last year?" Jon asked.

"Yeah, if you would like, I can bring the wheel chair up by your office as I leave at three-thirty."

"If it won't be out of your way to come to the East Wing, that would be great."

"I carpool with Mona who works in the East Wing. I'll just call her and tell her I will meet her at her office. OK?"

"Thank you, Jill, see you at three-thirty." Father hung up his phone and pulled himself up. He decided on another shower and non-cleric clothing for his evening out.

Promptly at four-thirty, Ramon pulled under the large canopy circle where patients and others often were picked up. Father Jon was sitting in his borrowed wheelchair with a big smile on his face. His cane rested across his lap.

The two men warmly clasped hands before Ramon started wheeling the chair to the car. "I did not know you were still in a wheelchair," Ramon quipped as he pushed Father Jon near the open passenger door.

"I'm not, when I am here, but the doctor wrote in his treatment papers that I had to have a wheelchair to go off campus." Carefully Jon pulled himself up from the chair and, using his cane, moved closer to the car. "I do think I could use some steadying, sitting down in the seat. This looks like a challenge."

"Sure," Ramon pushed the chair aside and partially lifted Jon until he was bent and into the seat.

"Thanks, put the chair in the trunk. I don't want to go off and have someone find it still sitting here." Jon smiled. It felt good to be in a car again.

Ramon looked sideways at Father Jon as he pulled out into the traffic. "Tell me, is there anything you want to see or do on our way to St. Ignatius. They are not expecting you until shortly before six."

"Could I see first-hand some of the sites that were damaged?"

"I sort of thought so. I planned a route that will cover most of them. We will also go by the

30

amusement park. It is really undergoing a radical change."

"Who owns it, now?"

"A foundation that is made up of city and private concerns. Most of the reconstruction has started, although the bridge will be at least two years before it can be finished."

Jon thought about those last days before he was injured, when five explosions and fires damaged the Cathedral, the bridge, a new downtown mall, a major telephone circuitry building and the pleasure boat on the river.

"Look!" Ramon exclaimed. He pulled into a small park on the edge of the river. "You can see the progress on the interstate bridge. They are still bringing up broken girders and cement column pieces."

"I thought the pleasure boat was burned." Jon was looking up the river.

"It was. That is the new one. Pretty, isn't she? She was donated by a city in the south. They had just bought her to replace their older one and decided to have her shipped to us instead. They received so many donations for the shipment that they were able to purchase another boat for themselves also."

Jon rolled up his window and looked at Ramon.

"Are you still at St. Ignatius?"

"Yes, there is much to do there, but you will see that later." Ramon continued, "Are you up to the ride out to the Cathedral?"
Jon nodded.

"They damaged the side altar, didn't they?"

"We'll just drive by it. Some other day, I'll take you into it."

"OK, drive on."

As they did a quick drive by of the Cathedral, Jon remembered his ordination there. That seemed to be centuries ago. How long ago was it? He tried to remember and finally quit trying. He guessed about ten years, but so much was still foggy for him. He became aware that Ramon had stopped the car.

"Are you alright, Father Jon?" Ramon was looking at him closely.

"I guess I was back somewhere in history," Jon smiled. "Where are we now?" Then he saw the entrance to the amusement park. The pedestrian gates were shut, but someone was opening the drive-in gate.

"Do you want to go and see what has happened to Spook Mountain?"

"Tell me first," Jon answered

"It is called Fantasy Mountain, and it is beautiful. Several of the boys have been working on it."

"Are they there now?"

"I don't know." Ramon signaled to the gatekeeper to keep the car gate open and slowly drove along the main concourse."

"The names have all been changed. None of those dark side names," Jon observed. When they got to the center park and picnic tables, Jon was clutching his cane.

"Look, Father!" Ramon pointed to the former Spook Mountain that now glowed in bright, pastel colors and sparkles.

"It doesn't look like anyone is working this late, it is after five." Jon stared at the building that was supposed to have been his death site. He found the change exciting. "No death in there!"

"No, but I seem to see two hitchhikers begging for a ride. Do you mind, Father." Ramon's teasing eyes gleamed as he pulled up beside two

32

clean-cut young men.

"Scar, William!" Father Jon wanted to jump out of the car and embrace them.

"You boys need a ride?"

They answered by pulling the backdoor open and climbing in to the car. Scar wrapped his arms around Father Jon and whispered to him, "I've missed you, Padre."

William leaned forward as Scar released Father and said, "You are our hero." Then embarrassed, he said, "Padre."

Ramon thrust a white handkerchief into Jon's hand. He pulled around the center park and drove back out of the concourse. The man at the entrance gate swung open the car gate and saluted them as they left. Jon didn't notice. He seemed to be having problems with his vision.

As they moved into the ghetto area, Jon noticed the construction going on. The previously called 'eyesore' building was undergoing considerable work. Ramon noticed Jon looking at it and said, "That building was discovered to be better built than most, and it will house all the burned out businesses. You can see the bakery is down at the corner. It is being leased to him for life at the cost of one penny. Some very grateful people in the area."

Jon nodded. He remembered the baker discovered the second arson fire early and, before it could take any lives, sounded the alarm, enabling those living in those buildings to get out. They turned down 3rd Street. It was wider, and traffic flowed both ways. He saw St. Ignatius Church. There was no chain link fence in front of it. There was a low stonewall, with grass and a couple of newly planted trees between the wall and the church. When he looked across the street to the other side, he saw new construction.

Suddenly, Scar covered Jon's eyes with his hands. "No fair peeking now," Scar said playfully as Ramon turned into the rectory drive. Scar removed his hands. "Look!" he exclaimed.

The driveway was covered with people welcoming him. Jon didn't know whether to cry or laugh. So many of them had come to see him at the hospital, and now they were gathered to greet him at the church rectory. Some were neighbors, both close and far in the ghetto, and some had lived with Jon through the tough days of fear and change at St. Ignatius.

"Do you want the wheelchair, Father?" Ramon was at his side.

"No, just assist me as I stand and keep my pathway clear. I will just use my cane."

A party had been arranged for those outside, while Jon was escorted into his old rectory. "Father Marvin, where is he?"

"Behind you," Father Marvin said.
Jon waited until he was inside before trying to turn around. That was one maneuver he was cautious about.

"You rascal, did you plan all this?" Jon asked as the two men hugged.

"No, they all did. I just had to wait until Dr. Forbes would let you come and for a favorable weather day at the same time. They were all so excited to have you come. The baker is catering it! Seems he is a bigger than life hero and he is organizing small businesses among the people. They will do anything he says."

Looking back on the evening after he returned to the hospital, all the names and faces that were familiar seemed to blend together. Jon was pleased when Patch rode back to the hospital with him. Ramon returned the wheelchair back to the

34

therapy area after delivering Jon to his apartment. Ramon and Patch stayed around a little while as they were aware of how tired Father Jon was from the surprise celebration. Jon called for an orderly to ensure he got into bed safely. All in all, the day had been exhausting.

The next morning, there were news clips of the impromptu celebration down at St. Ignatius. Jessie watched between bouts of severe leg pain. Sister Margaret Louise pointed out Father Jon. "You mean, the priest that acted as my advocate?" Sister Margaret Louise nodded. "Wow!"

Jon phoned and asked for a later therapy time. He was too exhausted to get up. A tap on his door, and Dr. Forbes came in. "A house call?" Jon quipped.

"No, but from all the publicity on television this morning about the priest from St. Ignatius parish, I figured you'd still be in bed."

"I'm dressed, but that is about the extent of my energies today."

"I'm not surprised," Dr. Forbes took Father Jon's blood pressure and frowned. "You really pushed yourself last night."

"And the night before," Jon murmured. Dr. Forbes looked at his famous patient. "I am ordering you off Chaplain duty for several days. I want you to rest, rest, and rest! Therapy told me you have figured how to get up off the floor by yourself. I don't want you doing that yet. And you were supposed to take a wheelchair with you last night."

"I did."

"Didn't see it in any of the pictures," the doctor said gruffly.

"It was in the trunk of the car." Jon smiled. "It would not have been as photogenic as just me and the cane. And it's hard to hug people from a wheelchair."

"I am ordering one up here for the next several days just to ensure you stay off your leg. X-ray will be coming to get you for some pictures. Be sure to smile," The doctor smiled at Father Jon.

"Jessie, the girl you worked on, can I go see her?"

"I understand Sister Margaret Louise is standing by with her. What did you do to Sister? She is there all the time."

"Just recommended she visit Jessie like she did me when I was first here."

"Wait a couple days before going up there. I am serious about you resting." Doctor Forbes was writing notes about his visit. "I don't want you to end up back in a hospital bed. O.K.?"

Father Jon nodded. "I will stay put and rest. Thank you for your care, doctor." The two men shook hands, and the doctor let himself out.

Jon rolled over in his bed and smiled as he let himself go back to sleep. Jon missed lunch. Awaking in the late afternoon, he was disoriented for a short while. Then he saw a copy of the notes scribbled by Dr. Forbes during his morning visit. Jon called therapy. Kelly answered. "I guess I missed my appointment this afternoon," he said.

"Dr. Forbes called and cancelled it. He said you needed your rest today after the big night last night. Did you know you were on the news last night and again this morning? There were reporters at that gala. Some gathering, huh?"

Jon laughed. "I didn't know I had so many friends. It was nice. I got to visit with the boys who had lived with me at St. Ignatius for a while. They are all doing well. So, am I scheduled for therapy tomorrow?"

"Let me check," Kelly said. Jon could hear

her turning the pages of the appointment book. "Yep, the usual time but if you decide to sleep in, give us a call and we will reschedule you for later in the day."

"Thanks, Kelly." Jon decided he was hungry. He nearly fell over the wheelchair parked outside his apartment door. Grinning sheepishly, he sat down in it and rolled himself to the elevator and on down to the cafeteria.

"Yo! Father, come sit with us." Jon balanced his tray with one hand and turned toward the voice. A group of interns pulled a chair away from the table so that there was room for his wheelchair.

"Can you do wheelies with that thing yet?" asked one of the interns.

"Here, let me help you." Melody, a pretty blond with remarkable blue eyes, deftly unloaded Jon's food onto the table and set his tray aside.

"You had a big night last night. Caught your picture on the news this noon."

"You were quite a hero," someone else said.

"I didn't know you were 'that' priest."

"So that is how you got your leg injured," another intern spoke.

Jon nodded his head and propped his cane against the table.

"Was that Sardoni man really going to kill you?"

"Will you hush! Maybe he doesn't want to talk about it."

"Or maybe I am having trouble getting a word in edgewise," Jon quipped.

The group laughed.

"And I haven't eaten all day," he said as he picked up his Hoagie sandwich. After he had eaten a few bites, he looked around him. Those who had already eaten were sitting watching him. "I guess I will have to autograph your napkins."

A collective groan and chuckle came from the group.

"Yes, Vincent Sardoni was taking aim at me when his life ended."

"He shot you in the leg?"

"Unfortunately, no." Jon smiled. "The bullet that killed Sardoni passed through him and ricocheted off the concrete sidewalk and hit my leg."

"What a bummer!" someone said.

"But, if that hadn't happened, you all would never have known me. What a pity that would have been." Jon had an impish look on his face.

"Yeah."

"I am off duty as Chaplin for about a week because of last night's gala at St. Ignatius. Dr. Forbes made a 'house call' to my apartment this morning."

"Ooooo! A house call?" There were grins all around the table.

"I didn't know doctors still did that. Sort of an ancient practice." Tom noisily slurped the last of his cola.

"Yeah, patients come to the doctors now, not the doctors going to see the patients."

Jon asked, "Does the President of the United States go to the doctor or does the doctor go to him?"

"Well, he goes to Walter Reid Hospital when he needs special help."

"But something like when he gets a paper cut or trips over something." Jon pushed the point.

"The doctor goes to him, but they have a clinic in the White House."

"And on Air Force One."

"So, I live in the hospital. Why should I go to see the doctor when he spends most of his time here?"

"You know, Father, this conversation is getting us nowhere."

Jon grinned as he scooped the last ice cream out of the plastic cup. "I know, but at least it allowed me to eat while you were thinking up reasons not to make house calls."

The group laughed amicably.

"Father, that young woman Dr. Forbes operated on is in my rounds. Is it true you asked Dr. Forbes to save her legs?"

"Not exactly," Jon paused, thinking about the event in ER when Jessie was admitted. "She asked for an advocate, and she was quite lucid and animate about saving her legs. I just happened along about the time she was looking for someone to 'stand in the gap' for her.

"That's scripture, isn't it? Stand in the gap." Jon nodded.

"It's something about a watchman on the wall and in the old Testament," Melody said.

"That's right," Jon commented. "Anyone know where that scripture is found?"

"What's this, a catechism class?"

"Is it in Ezekiel?"

Jon nodded. "What chapter?"

"I out of here," snorted one of the interns.

"Don't know," Melody answered.

"Look in chapter 22," Jon replied, "towards the end of the chapter."

With scraping of chairs, the group broke up. Melody picked up Jon's used dishes and trash as she left.

"We need to talk more about the Bible around here. There is too much reliance on what science can do." She tapped Father Jon on the shoulder. "You are good for us. Don't take anymore bullets!"

Sister Margaret Louise sat beside the now still Jessie. The girl had had a bad day of bouts of unrelenting pain. She finally had gone to sleep, but not before she again asked Sister Margaret Louise about the priest who had helped her keep her legs. They had watched the news clips about the gala held down at St. Ignatius. Jessie was surprised when she finally made the connection to her advocate.

"Sister Margaret Louise, they are calling from your room, wondering when you are coming back. It is time for your medicines." The nurse smiled at the diminutive nun. "Shall I tell them that you have moved in down here?"

"Oh dear, I didn't realize it was so late." Sister fussed with her walker. "Do you think she will sleep now?" She pointed at Jessie.

"I hope so. It has been a rough day for her. I can't imagine what kind of leg pains she is having. I will be keeping a close watch on her again tonight. Let's pray that she is stronger tomorrow. She hardly ate anything today."

"Father Jon's first few days were like this. And he only had one leg repaired." Sister answered.

"I remember, I was assigned to someone else but was aware of those first days. He was a good patient, and she is too. They both love the Lord."

Father Jon was enjoying his 'time off.' He was able to spend his freedom from official duties chatting with the various interns in the hospital. Their common complaint was that they did not get enough sleep, but, when Father quizzed them if they would rather be doing something else, the answer was always a resounding 'no'. He stayed in his wheelchair most of the days as he roamed the hospital.

He was in the cafeteria having lunch with Melody the second time that week. She had been up over twenty-four hours and was hoping to get some sleep shortly. She talked about the bad language some of the doctors used, especially in the operating room. Personally, she thought it was very unprofessional and she had noticed that some of the interns were copying the staff doctors. "Why are we like that? I mean, we always choose to go down, not up in our behavior?"

"Probably because of original sin," Jon answered as he scraped the last of the chili from his bowl. "Of course, that is too simple of an answer."

Melody nodded.

"We have free will, which God gave us. And it seems we prefer to choose the lesser than the greater behavior."

"That's the truth," Melody began to stack up the dirtied dishes. "Not many of them believe in God either."

"That is the main problem, I would suspect." Jon added his dishes to the tray Melody was working on.

"So, how do I witness to them?"

"First by not doing as they do."

"Oh Father, you know I don't say those things."

Jon smiled. "Prayer."

"What do I pray for, for them to stop their bad language? I don't think that will work."

"Have you ever told them that their language offends you?"

"No."

"Why not?"

Melody looked down at the table. "Probably because I am afraid of what they will say. And of course, I can't tell the staff doctors, not if I ever want to finish my internship."

"Let's pray together right now that they will

be struck silent anytime they start using that kind of language."

Bowing their heads, Father prayed. Melody agreed with a simple 'amen'. "Thanks Father, I'll let you know how it goes in surgery."

Jon nodded. He still had his ice cream to eat as Melody left, taking all the rest of the used dishes to the dirty dish conveyor. She waved to him as she left.

"Father Jon, Father Jon, please pick up a phone." The intercom interrupted his thoughts.

"I'm not on duty," Jon muttered as he wheeled himself over to a house phone.

A receptionist in the entrance lobby answered. "Oh, good, I couldn't get any answer in your apartment. There is a young woman here in the lobby wanting to see you."

"I was not expecting a visitor," Jon responded. "What is her name?" Jon could hear the receptionist talking with someone.

"Leah. She says she is your cousin."

"Ask her the first name of Grandma."

Again there was talking in the background. He heard the phone change hands. "Her name was Rosa, cousin Jon."

"I'll be right out, Leah. What are you doing here?"

"I'll tell when you get out here," Leah's voice teased.

Jon hurried back to the table where his ice cream was now mush. He tossed the plastic container in the trash and his used spoon into a disinfectant-soaking cylinder. He felt frustrated that he couldn't get his wheelchair turned around.

"Need some help?" Jon nodded at the candy striper. The young girl turned his chair expertly. "Where are you going?"

42

"To the Lobby, my dear one. Can you wheel me there? What is your name?"

"Barbara, and sure, that is where I am going too. Hang on and keep your feet up. We'll get there much faster if you cooperate."

"Thank you, Barbara, you handle this chair very well."

"My mother is in a wheelchair, so I have been doing this since I was eight years old." They were now in front of the elevators. She turned his chair around and backed it into the elevator when the door opened. "So much easier to get out this way."

"Can I pray for your mother?"

"Sure, her name is Karen. She has Parkinson's Disease."

The elevator door yawned open. "Keep your feet up!"

Jon did. He was eager to see his cousin, Leah.

"Meeting someone here?" Barbara asked. Jon nodded as he saw Leah striding across the room towards them. "Thank you, Barbara, here comes my cousin."

"Jon Mark!"

Leah was a thin young woman with taffy colored hair that flipped about her face as she reached down and hugged her cousin.

"How did you get here?"

"I was going to ask you the same thing, but I know how you got here."

"Let's go somewhere to talk," Jon said. "There is not much privacy here in the Lobby."

"Lead on, Jon Mark, I'll push. You just tell me where to go."

"I don't remember you being 'pushy' as a child," Jon laughed.

"Nope, sort of shy and serious, that was me. Turn here?"

"No, we'll go on down to the next visiting room. This one seems to be pretty full."

As the two cousins settled in a private corner of the next visiting room, they looked at each other and smiled.

"Now, tell me about you. Then we will talk about me," Jon spoke first.

Leah crossed her slim ankles and took a deep breath. "I am a missionary to a third world country. There are three of us who run an orphanage for HIV children. I am back here to try to get more help in the way of the medicines we need and financial backing. Now, you!" She grinned.

"Well, you knew I went to seminary to become a priest. Then after several assignments, I ended up here in a wheelchair, playing Chaplain when the doctor allows me. I am confined to the chair right now, but I normally walk with a cane."

"I couldn't believe it until I finally talked with Father Patrick when I got back in the states. I mean, you are a hero! But then you always did wear the white hat when we played as kids."

It was Jon's turn to grin. "The bullet was real. Those games we played as kids, when you got 'killed,' you just stood up again and kept on fighting with a new name."

"Yeah, and we did not have babies and people dying of AIDS either."

"Have you eaten lately?" Jon asked.

"An early breakfast so I could spend as much time as possible with you, Jonny."

"The 'Wayside Snack Bar' serves anytime of the day or night. This is a round the clock operation here. Give me a push and I'll steer you to the 'Wayside' now."

44

"OK."

"Actually, we will have more privacy in here," Jon said as they turned into the Snack Bar.

Although the Snack Bar was self-serve, one of the attendants came over to where Leah had parked Father Jon. "Father, what can I help you with today?"

Jon looked at Leah. "The submarines are good."

"OK, and a large glass of milk," She responded.

"And you, Father?"

"One of those special ice cream sundaes and water."

"Ice cream for lunch?" Leah probed.

"No, for dessert. It seems that I got a phone call about a visitor in the Lobby just as I was opening my ice cream in the cafeteria. It had melted when I got back to it. But no complaints, I'd rather have the sundaes they serve here." Jon looked at his cousin. He could see a depth that had not existed when they were teens. "How did you end up in a third world country?"

"Probably the same way you ended up being a hero. Something was missing when I was in college. After several false starts. I met Jesus. I finished my college work with a crash course in Third World Needs. I applied to serve. The long and short of it was that I ended up in a children's orphanage."

Jon nodded. "And HIV kids?"

The sandwich had arrived, and Leah took a bite. "Hmmm," she said.

"You are eating that like you haven't had a full meal for some days. Can I probe?"

"Sure."

"How many meals a day do you eat

normally?"

Leah held up one finger.

"Do you get paid for what you are doing?"

A shake of her head answered that question.

"So, why do you do it?"

Leah put her sandwich down and smiled. "Because they are God's forgotten children. Just because their parents have died of AIDS doesn't mean the children's lives are over."

"What kind of financial funds are you looking for? And medical aid?"

"We'd like to be better supported by individual churches than we are at present. It takes a fixed budget to keep a place going like Hope House. And as to the medical aid, we need a continual source of the medications that along with good nutrition often allows HIV babies to test negative after a year of two of life."

"Is there something I can do?" asked Jon.

"Yes, pray for us often. The local people are so afraid of these children that they sometimes abandon them on the garbage dumps." Leah looked down at her sandwich. "You would be surprised at the number of people who live on the dumps. Their houses are nothing more than cardboard or a sheet of metal and some plastic."

"Do you go to the dumps often?" Jon asked in a quiet voice.

"Not too often. There are a few of the natives who keep a lookout for the 'throw-away' babies and either bring them to us or tell us where we can find them. It works pretty well. We are so busy at Hope House just changing diapers and keeping the babies fed that we do not have time to go out and search for these children. Sometimes they are just left on our doorstep."

"After the shooting, I was given a large cash

46

award, probably because I survived it," Jon said wryly. "I placed it into the hands of the diocese for safe keeping. They take care of everything here, so I really have no need for the money. The Bishop has said that if I find a use for it, I can designate it to that use. I think I know how I would like to use it."

"Oh Jonny, I didn't come here to have you give money. I just wanted to share with you about what I am doing. Now, tell me about the shooting."

"Leah, dear, as your very best and closest cousin, I want Hope House to have the benefit of that money. Right now all it is doing is gaining interest."

Leah blushed and nodded acceptance. "Tell me how you got here."

"An evil man who hated the church and God was making life miserable for everyone," said Jon. He burned down whole city blocks at a time, killed when he wanted and decided I was in his way. I was at St. Ignatius Parish in the inner city and making disciples of a young teenage gang. First, he tried to get to them, but when they sought refuge within St. Ignatius, this evil man decided to drive me out, or in the end, to kill me."

"Well, I am glad he didn't succeed with the killing." Leah smiled. "I would have hated to find that you were dead already. But he did shoot you?"

"No, the bullet that killed him ricocheted off the pavement and splintered my thigh bone. It has slowed me down some, but one day I'll walk out of here with or without my cane and go back to living like everyone else."

"You said your thigh bone was splintered. How did they fix it, or did they?"

"A new revolutionary way of putting multiple pieces back together with a glue that eventually hardens like bone. The body doesn't reject the glue, but it plays havoc with pain at first."

47

"You were hurt about six months ago, weren't you? That is what Father Patrick told me. Does it still hurt?"

"Some, but mostly the leg is weak due to the extensive surgery to reconstruct the thigh bone. I may have been a hero out there but here, my doctor is the hero."

"I was shocked to find out that all that was going on in this city and reported in foreign news media involved you, my cousin."

"I was just following the Lord. Sometimes that can be less than popular. Or take a toll on you."

"Yeah, I know." Leah looked down at the last bite of her sandwich. "We have one worker who is testing positive for HIV now. They want her to return to the states for treatment. She doesn't want to go."

"That's not you, is it?" Jon asked softly.

Leah didn't look up when she answered, "No, but it could be so easily. It is sort of like living in a leper colony and caring for them. Your exposure rate is sky high." Leah's eyes were glassy with tears as she looked at Jon. "Mom and Dad want me to come home. They are afraid for me. I hate going against their will, but I belong over there. And if I someday test positive for HIV, I hope they won't abandon me. That is what happened to Lindsey."

"Jesus will never abandon you," Jon said softly. "He is your forever friend."

"I know." Leah sniffed. "I feel so stupid crying over Lindsey's rejection, but it is so sad."

"Do her parents know the Lord?"

"They say they do."

"Then I suppose we ought to pray for them to open their hearts to their daughter."

Leah smiled. "Yes," she whispered.
Jon reached across the table and took Leah's hands in

48

his as he began to pray for Lindsey and Leah and their respective family members. When he finished, Leah continued to smile.

"I didn't know I was coming here to be prayed for."

"The wheelchair doesn't get in the way of prayer. That is one nice thing." Jon signaled for the attendant. "Make up one of those sundaes for my cousin, please."

"Only smaller than the one he had," Leah added. "You know, I never have fresh milk or ice cream over there. All the milk is powdered. And ice cream is non-existent except in the large hotels that cater to the tourists. And, I might add, very expensive."

"Enjoy the treat." Jon grinned. "I remember how we used to share a fudge ice cream bar on the way home from school."

"Yes, and we almost got away with that until I got a big chocolate stain on one of my white blouses. Mom had a fit. She thought I was sneaking off with some boy."

"Well, you were." Jon laughed. "Only, the boy was your cousin!"

"I was afraid to tell her that because I thought you would get into trouble also."

"So then you started avoiding me, even though we both walked home every afternoon. I thought it was because I had acne!"

"You? I am the one who had the pimples. Eating those fudge bars probably didn't help the acne I had. Remember that horrible brown stuff all of us put on the zits to hide them. We were brown spotted freaks." Leah was giggling. "Remember the day you sat on a tube of that stuff and got it all over the seat of your pants."

"Yes, it took a long time to live that

49

nickname down!"

The ice cream sundae arrived. Leah dug in with gusto. "You'd think I hadn't had one of these in at least five or six years!"

"Has it been that long?"

"I think I last had ice cream at Grandma's just before I graduated from college. That was the first reunion when you weren't there. They said you were stuck at the seminary or something like that."

"That was the summer before I was ordained. We were. We didn't have many leaves that year. They were making sure we had given up everything, including family."

"That's a bummer, family is important!" Leah declared as she licked the ice cream off her spoon.

"The best family is the family of God; the one we are grafted into by Jesus."

"Yes," Leah smiled at her cousin. "Isn't it interesting that, although we are of different persuasions, we are both serving God to the fullest of our abilities?"

"Yeah, same God! I am proud to know that you and I are on the same team! And what I said about supporting the Hope House and the work you do with HVI children, I am going to do. Be sure to give me the information that I will need to see that the funds I have can go to that work."

Leah nodded. Her concentration was on the sundae she was eating. She had almost forgotten the sweet cool taste of ice cream and the addictive taste of the chocolate topping. She knew the memory of the sundae would remain with her a long time. Finally, she scraped the last of the dark chocolate syrup from the sides of the dish.

Jon was watching her intensity. "Will you come back to see me again before you go back?"

50

Leah smiled. "You really want me to come again? Before I came, I was afraid my beliefs and yours would clash." She dropped her eyes before looking up and staring earnestly at her cousin's face. "I didn't know what kind of reception I would get and all this." Her hand swept towards the wheelchair, "But, I am so glad I made myself come."

"You would have missed a terrific chocolate sundae, too," Jon grinned at her.

Leah blushed. "Yeah, that too."

"You will give me the information I asked for?"

Lean dug into her purse. She pulled out a folded piece of paper. "Here, I brought this just in case we were still able to talk about things."

The paper had her name and address at Hope House. She scribbled the name, phone number and address of the missionary agency she worked for on the back. "Call them and tell them what you want to give for the ministry at Hope House. You'll probably get Sarah. She was in a third world country until repeated bouts of dysentery forced her back for treatment. She lost part of her intestines to parasites. She is a brave woman, and if she wasn't 63, she'd go back overseas, whether her doctor said she could or not."

"She's your ministry hero?" Jon asked.

"Well, sort of. She has been a lot of encouragement when things get really rough. She taught one of the classes I took that last year in college. She was home on medical leave and so sick, but she insisted on teaching the class."

"She must have done a good job."

"Yeah, I was impressed. Of course, in college there are so many things that impress a college student. I hadn't known Jesus very long when I was in her class. I guess both Jesus and Sarah were a big influence."

Leah giggled. "I've talked a lot about me. Anything else you want to know?"

"No." Jon sat back in his wheelchair. "I think I would like to serve for a while in an underdeveloped country some day, but this leg will probably disqualify me."

"Not if that is what the Lord wants you to do. If He wants you there, you will be there." Leah glanced at her watch. "Oh my, where did the time get to? I'll have to hurry if I am to catch the train home."

Father Jon felt a keen stab of disappointment. He had not realized how much he had missed his cousin over the years, and to now find her serving the Lord with her whole heart thrilled him. He didn't want her to leave so suddenly. "Do you have to get back tonight?"

"I only took enough money to get a round trip ticket," she said with a sign. "I have to budget everything I do, and this includes what I spend while home raising money for when I go back."

"That is sort of hard, isn't it? Jon probed.

"Um, yeah. Like you have to spend money to raise money, and you never have enough for – let's say – a chocolate sundae."

"Let me call and see if one of the family guest rooms is available for tonight. Would you stay over?"

Leah thought of her responsibilities for raising money while her feelings warred for a few more hours with her favorite cousin. "I would have to call and let them know."

"Fair enough, let me make a quick call and check on a room. Then you can come to my 'apartment' and use my private telephone line to tell them you are staying over." Jon rolled his chair to the house phone and called administration. A few minutes later, Jon was all smiles. "There is one available. They said regretfully, it is in the East Wing. That happens to be the one on the hall I live on. It is in the administrative offices wing. Most families don't like that too much. No common parlor to meet with other families and family members."

Leah smiled. "I guess it is settled then. I was praying that if I wasn't supposed to stay, there would be no room."

"Must have been the wrong prayer." Jon quipped as he turned his wheelchair toward the exit.

"Can I push you?"

"If you want to get there in less than an hour, yes." Jon laughed and lifted his feet off the floor.

Following directions, Leah bumped the walls only a couple of times before they arrived outside of her cousin's apartment. "They call it an office studio. You'll see why when we get inside."

During the evening, Jon told her more details about the shooting that led up to his hospitalization. She shared stories of the children she had cared for. The evening went quickly.

After a late breakfast, Leah and Jon parted, promising to write occasionally. Jon rolled his wheelchair to the Solarium and found a corner where he could sit alone. For a long time, he let his mind go back over the conversation with his cousin. He smiled at the parallel of their lives. He thought about missionary work, but shook his head, remembering his injured leg.

He was deep in prayer when he heard a cry. "Someone, help me!"
Jon saw a lady bending over a man who was slumped in a chair. Jon pushed the panic button on one of the posts as he went by. "Can I help? I am a chaplain here."

The lady looked up with tears running down her face. "I think he has had a heart attack."

An orderly, followed by a nurse, had entered the Solarium. They spotted the slumped figure and ran to the man's side. Jon was praying over the man while the woman clung to the arm of the wheelchair. Moments later, after a quick assessment, a gurney arrived, and the man was sped off to the emergency room. Jon, holding the woman's hand, began the laborious task of wheeling his chair toward the hallway.

"Here, I'll help you," a voice came up from behind and began pushing the chair. All the while, Jon was speaking softly to the woman.

"He's dead, isn't he?" She said in her anguish. "They couldn't find a pulse."

After two turns, Jon pointed to the 'Staff' elevator. The person pushing grunted his response. Jon inserted his key and the door came open. "We can make it alright from here," he said to the one who was pushing. "Thank you very much."

"I was glad to help," came the reply as the elevator door closed on them.

"Push 'DOWN'," Jon instructed the woman. Seconds later, the door opened into the emergency room. Jon could see a great deal of activity going on in one of the cubicles.

One of the in-take personnel came up to them.

"The man who was brought down from the Solarium?" Jon asked.

"I'm his wife," said the woman, still holding Father Jon's hand.

The in-take personnel steered them toward a small office.

"I'll wait out here," Jon said to the woman as she nodded and released his hand before sitting on

54

the designated chair. A 'Ward Clerk' began to ask the lady questions.

Jon wheeled over to the main desk. "The man from upstairs?" A nurse nodded. "Is he going to make it?" The nurse looked over to the activity in the cubicle.

"We'll know in a few minutes." Jon felt the anguish that was in the ER room as they frantically worked on the man.

"Is that his wife?" The nurse glanced over at the small office.

"She says she is."

"Too bad," and the nurse ducked her head. "I wonder how long he was slumped there before she saw him."

Jon shrugged his shoulders.

"I thought you weren't on call this week. That is what is posted in the break room."

"You are never on leave when the cry comes in."

"Yeah, I know. Sometimes I even dream about patients arriving at my house by ambulance."

"Stress?"

"That, and the long hours." She looked back at the cubicle. "You are going to be needed." The staff was pulling equipment from around the now shrouded figure. "She is going to need help. I know those who can walk in and see death hit them and keep up. She can't."

"Experienced?"

"Too much."

A doctor came up to Father Jon. "Anyone with him?"

Father pointed at the small office. "A wife." Sighing, the doctor turned and walked to that room. Jon turned the wheelchair and began moving in the same direction. He could hear the soft murmur of voices as the doctor and woman talked. The Ward Clerk was clearly distressed. She was still holding her hands in ready above the computer keyboard.

"Father, she would like one of the Protestant chaplains to come down here."

Jon nodded and picked up a staff phone. His request echoed all over the hospital. Within five minutes, the Presbyterian chaplain was seated beside the new widow. Jon raised his hand in salute and began wheeling down the connecting hall that led to the cafeteria.

"Over here, Father," a voice called out. Someone took his tray, and Jon felt his wheelchair being pushed to a table of interns.

"We thought you were on vacation."

"No, just not on duty. Dr. Forbes decided I had had too much excitement on my one evening out and put me on leave."

"Yes, I heard him say something about keeping you out of a hospital bed." The cheerful smile of Melody helped lift his spirits.

"You were in ER just a little while ago."

"Oh, good golly, I've been caught!" Jon pretended he was a disobedient child. "You won't tell my doctor will you?"

"Well," said one of the interns with a mischievous smile, "not if you come clean with us and tell us what you were doing there."

Jon sighed. "Well, in that case, maybe I will and maybe I won't."

"It was confidential?" asked Melody.

"Not necessarily so." Jon answered.

"Well then man, what were you doing there?"

"His title is 'Father'," one of the other interns piped up.

Father Jon raised his hand for silence. "A

56

man slumped over in the Solarium. His wife called for help."

"Satisfied?" Melody's voice had sharpness to it.

The intern who had been in the ER finished, "The man died."

"Oh."

"Too bad," another said.

"Can't win them all," a third said.

"He was probably dead when his wife first noticed something was wrong."

Jon pulled his straw out its paper wrapper. "Life is sometimes so frail and surprising."

For once there was not a response from the interns.

"Have you ever considered that you might walk down the hall to respond to something and not complete that journey alive?" Jon looked at the group. "We never know what the next minute or second is going to hold for us."

Melody nodded. One intern left the table. The others seemed to be busy studying the floor.

Jon sipped his milk. The silence among the interns was almost unnerving. He thought about what he had said and decided, that given the same conditions, he would say it again. Finally, one of the interns cleared his throat.

"Father, the young lady who had the crushed legs is asking about you."

"Dr. Forbes has requested I stay away this week. I think he knows how involved I might get with Jessica. Isn't Sister Margaret Louise spending a great deal of time with her?"

"She practically lives down there. Do you remember all the hours she spent with you, Father?"

"Vaguely. It seems there was this constant pain and a nice little button to push to ease it. Only

57

thing was that I usually fell asleep then also."

"That pain machine is a blessing for the patient, the nursing staff and the doctors," one of the interns spoke up. "One order of the proper dosage of pain reliever and voila, no more hassles. One of the truly patient friendly gadgets."

"Maybe you ought to go into sales," one of the other interns laughed.

"Might if I can get through this year. At least I have seen what can be done and experienced the modern technology firsthand! Think what it would be like to be a doctor and selling this stuff. Might be easier than the long hours we put in otherwise."

Jon looked up. "Is that what you are looking for, something easy but that will make you money?" The boastful intern stared at Father Jon. "No, I really like getting my hands and clothing all bloody and covered with other peoples sickness!" His voice tone was scathing.

"Pardon me," Jon murmured. "I wouldn't have guessed." Jon pushed himself away from the table. "It is time I go take my nap."

Melody jumped up and took Jon's tray from him. "Let me take this. I'll push you to the East Wing as it is on my way."

The other interns all found reasons to vacate the table also, leaving behind only the intern who had spoken so rudely to Father Jon.

"You don't have to," Jon began, "but if you are going my way, it is speedier being pushed."

"Sure, Father, and by a blond, too!" Melody quipped with a grin.

Once in his room, Father Jon still sat in the wheelchair for a long time, praying for the angry intern specifically and for all the others who had been at the table. He wondered if he was supposed to be a Chaplain to the budding doctors or was his place just

58

with the sick, hurting and dying. Then he remembered all are dying, just some sooner than others. So what did that mean to that intern. The young man was probably angry about the inconsistencies of life and the hairline that is between being a doctor and being a patient. Only God knew when a person would be in need of a doctor or even would die. That had to be frightening for that intern. Doctors sure don't know this. They only come upon the scene after some illness or injury has created a patient-to-be for the doctor.

Jon finally rolled his chair over to his bed and with a little effort, moved to the bed. At least he could do this by himself. He closed his eyes, said a silent prayer for Jessica and fell asleep.

The good news on Monday was the freedom to return to active Chaplain status. Jon's first stop was in the nursery to check on the twin babies born to Mary Linden. He met the grandmothers who were fussing over each tiny child. A quick check in the post trauma area revealed Mary, smiling and getting ready to take her first trip to see her babies in the nursery.

Jon was smiling broadly when he arrived for his scheduled therapy. "Must be feeling better," quipped his therapist.

"Yes, two premies and their mother are healing after an accident caused an early birth. Grandmothers are thrilled over the babies, and, of course the recovering mother."

"I have news for you. Dr. Forbes wants a stress test on your leg before we continue with therapy."

Jon looked at Tony. "Is it going to hurt?"

"Not if what he suspects is true, that you are a lot further along in healing than he had hoped for."

"Was this enforced rest this week just to get

me frustrated?"

"Oh, I don't know about that, but Dr. Forbes was very adamant that you keep off your leg for a week." Tony grinned. We have scheduled ultrasound to be here so we can see what is happening when we stress your leg."

"That doesn't sound exciting." Jon laughed. "Can I pray while you are all doing your thing?"

"Please do," Tony said. His face took on a serious look. "Oh, here are the ultrasound techs. Hi, gals, how long will it take you to get set up?"

"As soon as we can get these cords plugged in," one of them said with a smile.

"Somehow, I feel like a condemned man," Jon ventured to say.

Dr. Forbes bustled into the room. "Someone is going to have to go on a diet. This room is crowded with all these techs and equipment."

"I'll leave," Jon joked.

"Over my dead body," Dr. Forbes answered. The doctor leaned over Jon and rubbed his arm with an alcohol pad.

"What are you doing?" Jon asked.

"Making sure you are completely relaxed while we are checking your leg." The doctor stuck a needle into Jon's arm. Within seconds, Jon was only aware of activity surround him, but no pain or stress. He closed his eyes.

A nurse and Tony were standing beside him when he awoke. "Welcome back, Father. The good news is that your leg is stronger than steel, or at least as strong as it was before you were shot."

"You're done?" Jon asked.

"With the stress test, yes; now onward with your therapy."

"My head is spinning, I think." Jon grimaced as they had raised him to a seated position.

60

"Take it easy, Father." The nurse cautioned him.

"Hmmm," Jon responded. "I'm going to be sick."

Later, an orderly rolled him back to his apartment and helped Jon into bed. He assured Jon he would be back to check on him in a little while. A tap on the door, and Dr. Forbes entered.

"Father, you weren't supposed to have a reaction like that!"

Jon looked at the doctor. "Must have scared you for you to be making another house call!"

"You can say that again. Whatever made you go unconscious like that? I only gave you a very mild relaxant."

"Well, doc, I relaxed in the arms of my Savior. The rest just happened." Jon looked at the doctor's face. "I really did scare you, didn't I?"

"Mmm." The doctor was checking his blood pressure and pulse.

The orderly had stayed discreetly in the outer room. "Do you need me to stay?" he asked.

Dr. Forbes nodded. "Until I send an aide to stay. Call your floor and tell your supervisor."

It was well into the evening before Father woke again. A nurse's aide was sitting beside him.

"Feeling better?" she asked as she adjusted the blood pressure cuff on his arm.

"I think so. I am going to have to get up and go to . . ." Jon waved towards the bathroom.

"Use the walker," she instructed as she helped him sit up. "Are you dizzy?"

"No, little light headed, maybe."

"Let me call an orderly."

Jon nodded. "Probably will be a good idea." He rested back in the bed.

Dr. Forbes arrived on the heels of the

orderly. "I've ordered a food tray from the cafeteria for you, and for an aide to be with you all night. By morning, you should be OK." He checked Jon's pulse and blood pressure again. "I've never seen that relaxant do what it did in you. I have a call into the drug manufacturer."

In the morning, Jon was back to normal, although Dr. Forbes had arranged for him to have his breakfast in his apartment. By ten, Jon was on his way to Jessica's room.

"Are you all right, Father?" the nurse asked as he checked in at the nursing station. "We heard you had a reaction yesterday?"

"News travels fast around here, doesn't it? Jon said with a grin. "I am up and walking, so I suppose I am OK. At least I'm not a patient again on this wing. How is Jessica doing?"

"Lots of pain, but her spirits are up. Sister Margaret Louise is with her most of the time. That woman is phenomenal, but you remember that from your stay on this floor."

Jon nodded his head but remembered that he really didn't recall much of the first couple of weeks. "Can I see her, Jessica, that is?"

"Sure, room 2117. Knock before you go in." There was no answer to Jon's tap on the door so he cautiously opened it. Jessica seemed to be sleeping. The miracle machine that fed pain relief into her stood beside the bed.

Jon crept nearer the young woman and gently touched her forehead with his oil-covered finger as he made the sign of the cross on her head. "Lord, look down favorably on Jessica and bring healing to her legs as you have done mine," he whispered.

Jessica stirred in her sleep and then opened her eyes. "Father!" she said.

62

Jon smiled at her. She closed her eyes again and was instantly asleep.

The light was blinking on the phone when Jon returned to his room. Housekeeping had been in and made up his bed and cleaned. That was one blessing of living as a patient in the hospital that he really appreciated.

Touching the answering machine, he heard the voice of Father Marvin. He hit pause and sat down in his recliner. Reactivating the answering machine, he listened to his friend inquire about his health and heard the general sounds of the rectory at St. Ignatius. It made him homesick. His short visit there a week or so before had stirred in him the feelings of being a parish priest again. Father Jon missed the constant give and take of parish life. Then he laughed at himself. Parish life had been stressful no matter where he had been. He wondered if he was destined to go through life always on the edge of some disaster. Somewhere, lost in these thoughts, Jon drifted off to sleep.

Jon wondered how long the phone had been ringing when he finally realized that his left elbow was ringing. He grinned at himself at that thought as he picked up the receiver. "Father Jon."

"Father, this is Emily on 5th floor. I have a patient that has requested you visit him. Are you able to come up now, or would later in the day be better for you?"

"I was napping. It will take me a little time to really wake up. I think I can be up there within thirty minutes. Would that be alright?"

"Sure Father, I thought maybe I had caught you at a bad time. I will tell Mr. La Costa you will be up here in a half an hour."

"La Costa? Is he related to the opera

singer?"

"He is the opera singer. He is in room 553."

"I am looking forward to meeting him," Jon replied before hanging up the phone.

He was a little stiff from his morning activities. The nap in the recliner had rested his mind but not his body. He pulled his walker from the corner before he tried to walk down the hall to the elevators. Fifth floor, he mused to himself. He wondered if La Costa was in one of the suites and why he was hospitalized. Jon realized he had not kept up with the news either on television or in the papers since his own injury. All kinds of things could have happened during this time period. He smiled to himself.

"Sorry, God, here I was putting myself first instead of where I should have my mind go."

The fifth floor could only be accessed from the east wing elevators. Just like a couple other floors that were restricted, fifth was reserved for patients who desired privacy or needed that privacy like he needed himself after he became famous for the end of the reign of terror that Sardoni had inflicted on the city. Jon waved at a receptionist in the admitting office as he went by.

The elevator doors opened with a whisper at the fifth floor. The walls were done in tasteful beige, with rich looking wallpaper in strategic places. The person who had endowed this floor stressed the requirement that it look less like a hospital. Hidden behind beautiful screens was the usual extra equipment that one found in many of the halls of the hospitals. The nurses were dressed in mute pastels colors. Their shoes made only muffled sounds on the expensively tiled floor. The ceilings were inlayed with panels of decorative sound proofing tiles.

Jon noticed the lack of the usual blaring

64

intercom. Then he saw the lights and remembered that they signaled that which normally you heard on the other floors. Every twenty feet there was a phone mounted in the wall that gave instant access to the intercom system. While he had been a patient on this floor, he recalled the serenity. Very quiet music was pumped through the discreetly placed intercom speakers. At the desk, he spoke to Emily. She gave directions to Suite 553.

"Anyone else there besides the patient?"

She shook her head 'no' and smiled. "I think that is why he wants to talk with you."

Jon could hear a voice singing. Its strength and resonance growing stronger as he neared number 553. He tapped lightly on the main door, and the singing stopped. "Come in," a strong, vibrant voice called out.

Sitting in the anteroom or front room of the suite was Philippe La Costa. "I would stand and prefer also to stand to sing, but I seem to lack the necessary energy at present. Thank you for coming, Father Jon Mark."

"Have we met before?" Jon asked.

"No, no, but you became famous in this illustrious city when I came to sing this time at the Opera House! Your name was on everyone's lips. I think I was a little jealous that there was someone more important than I." Philippe laughed a deep rumbling laugh. "I have a big ego, which I need to sing all those operas. Must not let the divas have all the spotlights or press. Sit down, Father, the chairs in this room are of finest quality and most comfortable. That often is a rare thing, quality and comfort in the same object." He emitted another rumbling laugh.

Jon chose a seat close to the great tenor. "Philippe La Costa, renowned tenor for the last twenty years. I am pleased to be of service to you if I can." Jon set his walker to one side.

La Costa's expression saddened. "Renowned but abandoned."

"Abandoned?"

"She left me."

"Who? Your wife?" Jon asked.

"Married for two years, a storybook love. I hadn't remarried after my first wife died because I was so afraid this would happen. You see, Marie, my first wife, was a jewel without comparison. But, after several years of loneliness, and Roselyn and I had known each other for many years; I decided to take a second wife. Roselyn had been good and attentive to me during these years and into this marriage until now." La Costa wiped a tear from his eye.

"Where is she now?"

"She went home. She has left me."

"Maybe you are mistaken. Maybe she went home for a short while."

"There is no mistaken!" Philippe pulled out a crumpled letter. "She wrote it all down."

Jon accepted the letter from Philippe's hand and read it. It indicated that his wife had left him and had flown back to Europe with no intent to return. "This is grave," Jon acknowledged.

"Why should I sing anymore? Why should I try to get well? She has left me and my life is over. I should not have married her but it all seemed so right after all these years." La Costa pulled out a big handkerchief and noisily blew his nose. "She says I am a has-been, and the only reason that they still hire me to sing is because of what I used to be."

Jon nodded. The words written in the letter were not that polite, but that was the essence of the missive in his hand. "The first thing we need to do is to pray for the writer of this letter."

"Pray what? That she will have a happy long

66

life? Oh for some of the poisons which are used in the great operas!"

"Philippe, poisons didn't cure the problems, you know that. Nor the daggers and self-inflicted wounds that left the heroine dying with great grace. If she is determined to leave you, she will. But first let us put your marriage to her on the altar of God and pray for her and you." Jon was surprised at the sternness of his words. "Your marriage was not something that is just thrown away because one or the other decides it was a mistake. You both knew the possibilities when you married. Even with the great differences in your ages, you had openly faced them, I am sure. You were married in the church, and I suspect the priest did bring up the differences." Jon continued, "She mentioned them in that letter. It is almost like she is challenging the church for letting you two marry."

La Costa looked down at his hands and twisted the wedding band on his left hand. "You read it. She says I railroaded her into this marriage." He swore quietly to himself. "It is like she was never a free agent but was forced to marry this broken down old man!" His words came out bitterly.

"Shall I pray, or are you willing to pray with me? Are you willing to pray for her and a solution to this dilemma?"

"I don't know," Philippe whispered. "I don't know."

Father Jon Mark moved from a seated position to one on his knees. He bowed his head upon the seat of the chair and began to intercede. Within moments, Philippe La Costa was beside him, bowed in prayer.

In a city in Europe, Roselyn La Costa sat in their attorney's office. "What are you thinking of?" asked the attorney.

"You heard me. I want an annulment of the marriage between Philippe and me."

"You have to be out of your mind! On what grounds?"

"I told you, weren't you listening?"

"I heard you. I thought you were trying to shock me. Over two years ago in this office, you signed an agreement with Philippe, acknowledging all that before Philippe would even talk with a priest about marriage. You can't just get an annulment just because you want to. Roselyn, what has happened?" Roselyn glared at the attorney.

"What does Philippe say about this?" Roselyn snapped her purse shut, and stood.

"Well, I see whose side you are on!" She walked out.

"Roselyn, wait! Let's talk about this."

Father Jon went by the Chapel to pray after leaving Philippe La Costa. He was dismayed by the simple acceptance attitude that Philippe seemed to have. Father Jon and Philippe talked and prayed together for several hours. Jon's stomach was complaining. He never had the problem before when he chose to pray and miss a meal. Must be something in the drugs, he thought that made him hungry at least three times a day. He gave up and went into the Wayside Snack Bar. He selected a deli sandwich and a frozen milk shake. The new clerk did not know what to do with his Chaplain ID card when he offered it up in payment. Jerry, the cook, came over and showed her how to scan it in just like a credit card. "Thanks, Father, for you business." Jerry saluted him and returned to the grill.

Jon went out into the courtyard by the snack bar and decided it was too windy to eat out there. He returned to a small table to finish his sandwich and

68

drink. Now that Jon had passed the stress test his doctor ordered, Jon's life became to take on an increasingly busy routine. He had his appointments channeled through the Telephone Receptionists in the hospital Lobby, as he seemed not to get back to his small apartment more than once a day to check on his phone messages.

During the following week, Jon spent hours with Philippe. The world famous tenor wrestled for days with depression at his wife's declaration.

Then there were the sudden calls for 'Father Jon' to the Emergency Room. All too often, these involved unexpected deaths or serious injuries. Jon was beginning to feel like a working priest again. He was content. Checking with the phone operator after a rather bloody accident had seriously injured two small children, he was startled to find that the Bishop had been calling him all morning.

"Jon Mark, here," Jon told the receptionist at the Chancery.

"One moment, Father, the Bishop is on another line. He has asked that you remain on the phone."

Jon made himself comfortable at the nursing station where he was calling from, picking up a pen, he absentmindedly clicked it open and close. One of the nurses pushed a notepad under the clicking pen and whispered, "Doodle while you wait."

Jon grinned and began drawing smiley faces. "Too noisy?" he mouthed.

"No," she responded. "Just takes the stress off."

"Thanks for calling, Father Jon. You are doing well now?"

"Yes, your Excellency. No more scares and lots of activity here."

"I want to see you this afternoon. I have

contacted the hospital administration that we shall need one of the Conference Rooms. I will be there at 2:30. I think we will be meeting in the Purple Room. You can find out from Administration. You can be there at that time, Father?"

"Of course, your Excellency. Anything I should particularly know about this meeting?"

"I have been in touch with a Bishop in Europe about a certain famous tenor currently in residence at the hospital. I don't suppose you have met him."

"Oh, but I have. He has been discussing his problem with me for about a week."

"Good," replied the Bishop. Then we will not have to go over so much if he is talking with you."

"Yes," Jon said. "He is quite depressed over the situation."

A quick milkshake proceeded Jon's prayer time in the Chapel. He had finally given in to the need to keep his stomach pacified. He looked around the small room and thought about the various religious objects in the room. The hospital, in attempting to keep the chapel as a neutral prayer room, had removed the most obvious Catholic and even Christian symbols. They were locked in the small closet just inside the door, so if someone really did want them visible, they could be brought into the room. It irritated Jon that the hospital was falling victim to the masses instead of leading the people to the source of their healing and life. He decided he would bring this divorcing of faith and the hospital up sometime soon to the Administration. Maybe he could enlist the Bishop's influence in the matter. For that matter, he missed celebrating Mass everyday. He hadn't had the strength at first, but now it was an empty spot in his life. He could go across the street

70

to the convent chapel, but they had a priest who was assigned to meet their needs.

"What about the needs of the people here, Lord?" Jon uttered aloud. "They want a Chaplain at their beck and call, but they are afraid to live their faith in front of each other."

He thought of the ridicule Sister Margaret Louise suffered for her faithfulness to a pure life of service and compassion. Jon shook his head. "They probably say things behind my back, too, especially with those interns that Melody hangs around. And probably about Melody too." Jon checked his watch. It was a little after two. It would take him about twenty minutes to negotiate the walk to the Purple Conference Room. He sighed and picked up his cane before leaving the room.

The Bishop and Chancellor arrived just after Jon got to the room. Accompanying the Bishop was one of the diocesan attorneys and another man who looked like he might also be an attorney. After a short private greeting between Father and the Bishop, they all took seats at the table. The second man was an attorney who dealt with international law. The Bishop looked at Jon. "You are looking well."

Jon nodded his thanks. He wondered what this meeting was all about. A commotion outside the door announced the entry of Philippe La Costa. He was introduced to the attorneys, who then got up and left the room. The Bishop nodded to the Chancellor, who also left.

"My son," the Bishop began looking at La Costa. "You are aware of the charges made by you wife?"

"Yes, I have been discussing them with Father Jon Mark. They are without basis. I do not understand them or her position. I am devastated."

"Since she has decided to involve the church

in this issue, I have asked the attorneys for this diocese to research the complaint."

"Isn't this under the seal of confession?" Father Jon asked.

"I wish to God that it were, but his wife has made it public."

"You didn't tell me that." Jon said, looking at Philippe.

Philippe dropped his eyes. "I am sorry, Father Jon, I had hoped it would all just go away like a bad dream."

"These kinds of things never do," murmured the Bishop. "So, is there any truth in them?"

"No, I swear that I have never done any of those things that she is telling about. So help me God."

"This confirms Philippe's confession?" the Bishop asked.

Jon inclined his head slightly.

The Bishop continued. "The way it appears is that your wife, for some unknown reason, has taken a lapse of memory of truth. She seems to have something against the Catholic Church that probably has nothing to do with the stories she is telling now." Philippe nodded. His voice broke as he tried to speak. The Bishop held up his hand. "No need to try to figure it out, Mr. La Costa. There is so much hatred in what she is saying that only God knows how to reach her. You and Father Jon Mark have been praying for her?"

"Yes," Philippe managed to whisper. Father Jon nodded his head.

"Because you are presently living within my diocese, your Bishop Anthony Garnova has asked that I extend whatever ministry to you that is necessary. I have taken the steps to have the attorneys check into the liability and slander of your

72

wife's statements. They directly reflect upon the church in such a way that, although the church will not press a suit against her, we will stand in defense with you. Some people may find that surprising, but I rather think that is what Jesus would do." The Bishop smiled. "You have Father Jon Mark to thank for that novel idea; that is doing what is just and right rather than what we would normally do that would not cost us any harm."

Father Jon felt his ears get warm at the unexpected compliment.

"Are you sure that you want to get the church involved?" Philippe asked. "I am not a poor man. I can mount up a defense."

"But would you?" asked the Bishop. "Our support will encourage you and maybe discourage another from doing what your wife is doing. And we need to think of everyway we can possibly reach her and get a dialog going that might free her from this terrible bondage she is in. That is the ultimate goal of our prayers and support."

"I can agree to that. Roselyn was a fine lady until the accident at the opera house that night. Not only did I nearly break my arm when I fell, but this ugly gash that cut across my face has deformed me. I am ugly. Who would ever let me back on stage to play anything but the 'Hunchback of Notre Dame'!"

"How did it happen, the accident? I read the article in the paper but I have forgotten the details." The Bishop looked at the great tenor.

"A cable, a cable that wasn't there during rehearsal! I tripped over it as I was making my exit from the stage. The lights were bright on stage, but it was dark where I had to go. I didn't see it. I fell, and my face and throat were ripped open by a piece of costume armament. It just missed slicing my vocal cords." Philippe lifted the lower edge of the bandage

73

on his neck to reveal a red scar crossing his throat.

"But it didn't," Father Jon said quietly. Philippe and the Bishop looked at the priest. "I have heard you sing since the accident."

La Costa nodded. "I think that is what has saved my sanity at this point. I still have my voice."

"So," the Bishop's voice was soft and compassionate, "What are you going to do with that voice."

"I don't know," the cry came from Philippe, "I don't know!" He held his hands over his face and sobbed.

"Plastic surgeons can take care of the facial scar and the one on the neck, but you going to have to let God heal the one in your soul."

Later that evening, Father Jon picked up his phone and called his friend, Larry Janski, the detective. Larry's wife answered. She was delighted to talk with Father and said her husband had just gone out to do something in the flowerbeds for her. Within minutes, Larry and Jon were comparing old times with each other and what each was doing now that Larry was no longer in the precinct that covered the area of St. Ignatius.

"I have a favor," Jon said.

"Didn't figure this was a social call," Larry laughed. "Someone steal your cane, or are you still using the walker? I heard that your doctor put you on 'house arrest' right after that shindig at the rectory."

"Mostly, I use the cane but on bad days the walker is handy to lean on," Jon retorted.

"So what is the favor?" Larry asked.

"Do you remember about a month or so ago, Philippe La Costa took a fall back stage at the opera?"

"Yeah, nearly broke his arm and got cut pretty badly on some decorative costume armament."

74

"OK, you've got the right event. Suppose the fall was set up to maim or disable La Costa from ever singing again. Could it have not been an accident?"

"Hmm. It wasn't considered that night, but I do remember the investigating detective commenting on how irate La Costa was once he discovered he still had a voice. He thought it was the nature of the man and didn't give it too much consideration as to why La Costa fell. Do you know something different?"

Jon laughed. "Would I call you just to bring this topic up and not have an idea of something?"

"No," Larry laughed also. "It was not a backstage 'accident'? Is that what you are trying to say?"

"Let's say that maybe someone intended for him to fall and be seriously injured, or maimed."

The following morning, after an exhausting therapy, Father Jon was visiting in the cancer wing. St. Elizabeth's had a state-of-the-art cancer facility. The aggressive but compassionate treatment often sent seemingly hopeless patients back to their families. He heard his name called out from the room he had just passed. Turning, Jon walked back a few steps. Pastor Rudy White was standing in the door.

"What are you doing here?" Father Jon blurted out before he could check himself.

"My mother." There were tears in the black pastor's eyes. "Would you come in and pray with us?"

Jon bear-hugged his friend. "Certainly, that is part of my job description."

"Who is it?" A diminutive dark lady asked from the bed.

"Mother, this is Father Jon Mark from St.

Ignatius Parish. Some of his boys have been attending classes in our education building. And you know the doctor and his wife whom we gave shelter to after the buildings burned last year. He sent them to us after second the fire."

The petite lady vigorously nodded her head. "I don't see very well anymore. Won't you come closer?" She extended a thin bony hand out from under the blanket covering her.

Jon grasped the hand that was surprisingly strong. "Mrs. White?" He glanced at Rudy to confirm that his mother's name was 'White' also.

The elderly lady noticed the hesitation. "Yes, I am one of those who still has the same last name as her kids."

Jon Mark grinned. He thought he had been not so obvious. "You're quick," he teased her.

"Mother, Father Jon is as close to being godly as any man I have ever met."

"You haven't looked in the mirror much lately then, have you?" the old lady snapped back.

Jon grinned again. "Family resemblance? With Christ? Multicolored?"

Rudy chuckled.

"You're my boy, and I raised you right. You're darn right there ought to be a family resemblance." Mrs. White retorted.

"Would you pray for Mother, Father Jon? This hospital has a way of producing miracles and we certainly could use one. The doctor's are less than happy with Mother's progress."

"That isn't my fault, son. It just may be God's will that I am to go 'home' to Him soon."

Rudy's face was etched with grief. Father Jon pulled out his bottle of anointing oil and said, "May I?"

"Of course," Rudy answered.

76

"Do what?" Mrs. White snapped.

"Anoint you with Catholic anointing oil," Rudy replied.

"Anoint away!" the old lady responded.

Jon made the sign of the cross on her forehead before praying. He offered the bottle of oil to Rudy, who also anointed his mother. Together they prayed.

Mrs. White did not move after they had finished. She had her eyes shut and a serene expression on her face.

Jon hugged his friend again. "Call for me anytime. I live here in the hospital and can be here very quickly."

"You're a nice man," Mrs. White murmured softly. "I am glad you are Rudy's friend."

After several more stops to visit with patients, Jon made his way back to his apartment. He stopped to pick up a milkshake at the snack bar. The answering machine light was blinking. Jon settled into the recliner before punching the button. The first call was from the Bishop's office about his request to send money to the Hope House, the ministry where his cousin was working. Jessie was the second call. She asked if he would come see her soon. Sister Margaret Louise also had called with the same request for Jessie.

Jon sipped at his drink and prayed for those he had just visited. Two were not going to survive their cancers unless God intervened. Jon reminded the Lord of his faithfulness for so many and asked that again the so called 'miracle recovery' would be visible for these patients also. One in particular worried Jon, for the patient had given up hope of recovery. He also had expressed doubt that God cared. Jon had shared the Biblical truths with that patient. Down deep, Jon feared the man was rejecting any relationship with the Lord.

Jon felt almost depressed as he thought about the personal needs in various parts of the hospital. He remembered Philippe La Costa and his physical and emotional scars. Somehow he wanted to get Philippe involved with some of the other patients in the hospital while the surgeons were mending the scars on Philippe's face and neck. Money did buy something, and Philippe was going to stay put in the hospital until his features were restored to some normalcy. Sort of like using the hospital for a sanctuary as the gang did with St. Ignatius. An interesting thought.

Then there was the problem of Sister Margaret Louise. She did have cancer and was adamant about not pursuing chemo or radiation therapy. He had spoken with the Mother Superior of her order about the situation. She was free to move back into the convent anytime, and they would care for her until her death. When he had shared that with Sister Margaret Louise, she just looked at him with a far away look on her face and a slight smile. She told him she would when she was no longer useful for Jessie.

Jessie was making progress. She was trying to walk with a walker. The muscle damage to her legs was so extensive that she had to have braces all the way up her legs to her waist. She had guts though, considering the amount of pain that still racked her extremities day and night. The extensive pain was a concern for Dr. Forbes. Jon had not visited with Jessie very much because of other needs in the hospital, and of course, there was Sister Margaret Louise always available to the young woman for emotional support.

Jon realized he had fallen asleep while praying when his pager went into its second level of alert. He looked down at the screen. ER! He headed to the elevator as fast as his leg would let him. He was only using the cane today, so he had to pace himself. It would not do for him to fall because he was careless in his hurry.

As the door popped open in ER, he could see a commotion in one of the patient rooms. He glanced at the desk and realized no one was behind it. "Oops." Jon muttered to himself and moved toward the disturbance in Room 8.

"Glad you are here, Father," a voice spoke from the far edge of the room. "We seem to have hit an impasse for treatment for this young woman. She is claiming Catholic reasons for refusing to let us help her."

Father Jon nodded. The several nurses, aides and other personnel left the woman's side and slipped out beyond the curtain. A small young girl, probably no more than thirteen or fourteen, looked at the priest. "Are you really a Catholic Priest?" she asked.

"Yes," Jon replied, "and you have a name?" "Joanie."

"How old are you Joanie?"

"Eighteen."

"Truthfully?" Jon tried to make eye contact. Joanie looked down, refusing to meet his eyes.

"Yes," she answered. "You don't believe me, do you?"

"Is that your purse?" he asked. "Do you have a driver's license?"

"Yes, and don't touch it."

"Because you really aren't eighteen?" Jon looked at the small figure draped with just a sheet. "Are you cold?"

Joanie nodded. Jon pulled a blanket off the end of the gurney and laid it over the girl. She was obviously pregnant and pretty far along.

"When is the baby due?" he asked.

"Don't know," she sobbed.

"Do your parents know?"

"No, and you can't make me tell them."

"So you are not living at home, right?" Jon shifted his weight to his stronger leg.

She only nodded and tried to sniff back her tears.

"Are you Catholic?"

"No," she whispered. "I only told them that so they would not try to take the baby away from me."

"Like abortion?" asked Father Jon.

The girl sobbed. "He tried to kill the baby."

"Who is he?"

"Charlie."

"Does Charlie have a last name?"

"He never told me."

"Why at this late date," Jon indicated her bulging stomach, "would he try such a thing?"

"You don't understand. I live on the streets."

"Oh yes, I do understand. I used to work in a ghetto. Girls like you were plentiful."

"What are they going to do to me?"

"I don't know until you let a doctor look at you. How did you get here? Did you just walk in the ER door?"

"No, they dumped me on the street, and one of the other girls brought me here."

"Where is she now?"

"She left when she got me inside the door. She doesn't want them to know she brought me here."

"I can imagine," Jon said.

Joanie was now crying almost uncontrollably.

"What can I do for you Joanie?" Jon asked.

80

He rested his hand on her arm. Do you want me to pray? Do you want me to talk with the nurses and doctors? You do realize as soon as they examine you, a police report will have to be made. Do you want your parents?"

"Can they take care of me without my parents knowing? They'd die if they knew what was happening to me. They hate me. They didn't care when I left."

"Did you tell them you were leaving?"

"No. I just didn't come home from school one night."

"Don't you think they would be glad to know you are alright?"

"Yeah, alright but pregnant and bleeding. What a way to be alright!" Her voice hardened. "They won't ever forgive me."

"Why, because you don't want them to or because you can't forgive yourself?"

"What do you mean? Forgive myself? Why would I have to do that?"

"Well, if you don't, it probably means that you hate yourself for what you have done and become. Does that make any sense, Joanie?"

"Yeah. I hate everybody and I hate myself! Nobody has ever cared about me."

"I do," Jon answered softly, "and so does God."

Joanie started to say something but suddenly moaned in pain instead.

"You need the help of the doctors and nurses here. Will you let them help you?"

A nurse had put her head in between the curtains. The pain in Joanie seemed to intensify, and she let out with a scream. A doctor and another nurse appeared.

"Joanie! Let them help you. I promise they

will not do anything that is immoral or illegal to you."

Joanie nodded and screamed again in pain. A nurse stuck her with a hypodermic. Within seconds, Joanie was unconscious.

"Will you sign for her Father?" Jon nodded. "Someone has to, and I seem to have been down this road before." Jon scribbled his name on the admit paper. "Do we have any idea what her real name is?" "Check her purse. Might be a clue there. They usually don't come in with any ID, but you might get lucky." The doctor and nurse were examining the unconscious girl. "She's going to need surgery fast, and blood."

"Don't tell me you are going to need 'O positive'," Jon quipped.

"With the meds you are on, you're disqualified for now. God is with you today!" The doctor grinned.

The nurses now had the gurney moving toward an elevator.

"Take the purse, Father, otherwise it goes into security lock-up, and she might never find it again."

Father Jon grabbed the purse. "Will you page me when she is out of surgery?"

"Sure, Father, and maybe a mother too! The baby is alive, but we don't know how damaged. Good luck locating parents."

Jon muttered to himself all the way down the hall until he found a quiet place to look in Joanie's purse. The usual girlie stuff was in there, no ID, but then he felt something in the lining on the bottom. Carefully, he pulled rough stitching apart and pulled out a letter. It was address to a Mr. and Mrs. located in a neighboring state.

"Maybe parents," Jon whispered to himself.

82

He stopped behind an appointment desk and picked up a hospital tote bag. When the clerk looked at him, he grinned. "I don't want to be seen carrying a 'purse' around here. Too many misconceptions would pop-up."

"I won't tell," the clerk replies.

In his apartment, Jon prayed before opening the sealed letter. 'Dear Grandma and Grandpa', it started. "Eureka!" Jon hollered as he reached for his phone.

"That number is unlisted," the mechanical voice said.

Jon thought for a moment and then phoned Detective Janski. He would know how to circumvent the unlisted number problem. Larry Janski was on another line.

Jon's pager went off. It was from surgery. He called the number and heard the doctor say, "A preemie baby boy, some cuts on his face and head, but they do not look drastic. I am sending him on down to the preemie nursery. Baptizing him might be a good idea. Girl is cut up inside. Whoever tried to abort the child sure didn't get much of a chance. She has cuts all over her, indicating a pretty good fight on her part." The connection went dead before Jon could say anything.

Father Jon made a quick call to the front desk to keep trying to reach the Detective Janski for him. He hurried to the preemie nursery. He knew the routine now, grabbing a gown and mask as soon as he came in. "Wash you hands!" came the gruff order from behind a facemask. Jon pushed the liquid sterilizing lubricant button and dutifully scrubbed down his hands.

He stepped over to the nurses cleaning the new baby and saw the cuts on his face and head. One of the nurses looked up with tears in her eyes. "Poor feller, almost didn't get the chance to be here." She handed the baby and a bottle of sterile water to Father Jon. She made the sign of the cross and bowed her head as he baptized the boy. As she took him back, she said, "What name did you give him?"

Jon grinned, "John, of course."

As soon as he hit the hall, his pager went off. He briefly thought about the doorbell at St. Ignatius that always rang when he was busy. Jon hurried into another wing before answering the page. "Your call to Detective Janski has been completed, and he said to call back as soon as you were able."

"Detective Janski, soon-to-be-retiring" came his friend's cheerful voice. "How are you, Jon?"

"When I get through doing the laps around here, I will be ready for the Olympics, the elderly Olympics that is."

Larry laughed. "Got you hopping, huh? Leg must be doing OK."

"I need to contact a couple in the next state who have an unlisted phone number. Can you help me? Their granddaughter is in surgery right now. She is a run-away and until a short while ago, pregnant. There is a preemie boy in the nursery now."

"Name, address?"

"I left that in my apartment when I hurried to the nursery to baptize the little guy. I named him 'John'."

"Figures. OK, call me when you get to your apartment. I will keep my line open for you."

Twenty minutes later, Father Jon was talking to very tearful grandparents. They told Father that their granddaughter. Linda Sue, had been missing for about seven months. They gave him the phone number for her parents and said they would start for the city and St Elizabeth's Hospital immediately.

84

The woman who answered the phone at the number Jon was given was suspicious of the caller. Jon repeated his identity several times until she finally understood that he was 'that' priest who had nearly been killed last year. He told her what he had told the grandparents and asked if she could come to the hospital. "My husband is out on his delivery route."

"Can someone bring you in?" he asked again. "Your daughter is going to need her mother."

Again there was hesitation. "This is a one person office. We run a very small operation, but a successful one."

"Can you reach your husband? Does he have a cell phone, or radio with him?"

"Yes," she said. "Only, he is out-of-range right now, down state."

"What is the number or call letters? I can arrange for someone to reach him." Jon wrote down what she said and repeated them back to her to make sure they agreed. "OK, get ready to close your office. I will see that you are picked up by a police officer in your community. They will pass you on from district to district. When you get to the city, an officer by the name of Larry Janski will be your escort into the hospital. In the meantime, we will try to reach your husband.

"OK," the timid voice replied. "I'll start closing down."

"Larry, here is the battle plan." After explaining about the police escorts needed and the father to be reached by radio, Jon continued. "I obligated you for the last escort into here. I think we will need a compassionate police officer here when everything comes to a head." Father Jon laughed when Detective Janski said that he'd get even someday.

"I already owe you for my life. What more do you want?"

Detective Janski laughed in return, "See you later!"

It was late before the reunion between daughter and parents and grandparents and the new baby was accomplished. Emotions ran high all night. Father Jon was grateful that he had asked Larry Janski to be the police representative. Larry superbly handled the attempted abortion/murder of the unborn child and talked everyone into a speaking relationship. Jon spent a few moments in prayer for the family situation before dropping off to sleep near dawn.

There was a confab in the cafeteria a few days later when Father, using only his cane, arrived. Melody scurried to his side at the tray rail to assist Father with his tray. "Glad you are here, Father," she said brightly. "We are in an intense discussion about what to do about the budget cuts that were announced last night."

Jon raised an eyebrow. "I guess I missed something. Are they severe?"

"Not funding the orthopedic special unit that will continue Dr. Forbes' work is one of them!"

"This sounds serious." Jon sat down in the chair another intern had pulled up to the three tables now nestled together with interns and a few last year nursing students.

"It is, Father. The hospital seems to think that a new Atrium and a parking garage is more important than a unit that specializes in bone repair such as yours or that young woman, Jessie!"

Jon looked around the tables. "Is that the consensus of all of you?" Most heads nodded, but a couple shook their heads 'no'. "You seem to disagree." Jon was looking at one of the nursing

86

students. "Why?"

"There are cuts in all the departments. I thought I might have a chance of hiring on here after I graduate because of the needs here, and the previous budget was generous in salaries for nurses in my specialization. But that is cut also."

Nodding, Jon looked at the intern who had shaken his head 'no'. "What areas concern you?"

"They are not funding any of their satellite clinics next year. If the clinics stay open, it will be on a shoestring budget. What kind of health care is that for the people that need it out there?" He waved his hand wildly towards the windows.

"Anybody know the reasons for the cuts? How about you, Father, will your job be cut too?"

Jon shrugged his shoulders. "The Diocese will pick up my tab, I imagine. Anyway, you all know I work for nothing." There was a wave of chuckles around the table.

"Yeah, and 24/7, too," someone added. "You were down in the emergency room until after 2 o'clock a couple of nights ago and back in pediatrics before 6 o'clock the next morning."

"How do you know?" someone challenged. "Cause I was there too."

"How is that child?" Jon asked.

"The young girl or the baby? She'll make it, no thanks to her parents. She is terrified of them. Social Services have already staked a claim."

"Do I need to contact them, Social Services?" Jon asked

"I think they have everything they need. I wrote a scathing report about the behavior of her parents, as did the Triage Nurse in ER. They know you were there, so they'll contact you if they need you."

"I am glad something is being done for the

girl. I have prayed for her every day."

"Back to the budget cuts, you guys." Heads nodded, but no one spoke.

"Are we going to just sit here and let them do it?"

"What else can we do?"

Father was opening his carton of milk. "Maybe you ought to get all the facts first. What is really being planned and who is being budgeted out of this hospital. Try to get a copy of the report as it was issued yesterday and make copies for all of you."

"And one for you, Father?"

Jon thought a minute. He could get a copy without suspicion in the hospital administrative offices, but it was possible that that copy and the one the interns ended up with would differ. He had noticed that over the last half year. "Yes, one for me too."

"I'll get a copy," one intern said as he picked up his tray to leave.

"I will see that copies are made," one of the nursing students offered.

"Then what?" The question was almost belligerent in tone.

"We'll meet tomorrow and discuss what we have learned." Father Jon took the lead.

"I'm on 24/2 starting tonight at six," Melody said to Father, "so I won't be in the loop for any discussions."

"We'll keep you informed," one of the other interns promised.

Jon moved slowly down the hall. He had a copy of the proposed budget for the next fiscal year in his hand and a copy of the budget for this year. "I hear the interns are all upset about the proposed budget," one of the clerks in the Administration Office commented.

88

Jon nodded. "That's why I wanted to see these."

The clerk leaned forward over the counter and said quietly. "It isn't only the interns who are upset!"

Jon studied the budget plan carefully. Money and budgets were not Jon's strong suit, but he recognized the differences between the current budget and the budget proposed for next year. He did some tallying and realized the large number of jobs being cut or reduced. There was the item for the second parking garage. Jon knew it was becoming a critical need for the hospital. The item about the Atrium was not for a new one but for repairs and revisions to the floating walls and the heating and cooling system, plus a permanent groundskeeper. The amount was staggering. He knew that volunteers did that work now, with the custodial staff picking up the loose ends. Even so, that entry made a lot of sense as Jon knew how appreciated the Atrium was by both patients and visitors. Sometimes those in grief from the loss of a loved one preferred to sit and talk in the Atrium rather than the Chapel or an office.

Jon was still thinking about the budget changes when he went up to see Jessie. He was making it a point to spend time with her everyday. As they talked, Jon became aware of the very spirited young woman who daily was coping with learning to walk again and enduring on-going, nearly continuous leg pain. He admired her greatly.

"You're somewhere else, Father," Jessie probed as the silence grew between them. "What are you thinking about? I don't mean to pry, but you didn't finish that last sentence." She had a slight smile on her face. "Is it something I have said?"

"No, Jessie. You are right, I am somewhere else in my thinking." Jon looked at her, toying with telling her about the budget cuts. Would that be talking out of turn to say something about that to a patient? Maybe. He spied the in-house newspaper on the chair next to Jessie's bed. "Anything of interest in that?" He pointed at the paper.

Jessie laughed. "They printed the budget in such fine print that you have to have excellent eyes to be able to read it."

"Which you do," Jon retorted. "You haven't read it yet, have you?"

Jessie smiled. "Is that what is bothering you, Father, the budget for next year? Hopefully neither of us will be in here then."

"Then you have?"

"Yes, I am glad that since I had to end up with broken, crushed legs, that it was this year and not next."

Jon felt a spark of an idea beginning in him. He looked at Jessie. "Didn't you tell me you worked as a promoter of events?"

"Yes, I used to work for HH&W Promotions and had just started an agency of my own when this happened," and she wave her hand towards her legs.

"Then you know how to raise money?"

"Like on a farm?" She said with a twinkle in her eye. "I haven't learned how to raise it in a garden yet."

Jon laughed with her.

"But to promote something, yes, I know how."

Jon sat back in his chair. "It might work," he said softly to himself.

"Father, what are you thinking about? There, I have asked you again. Can you share?"

"A little later, Jessie. I have an idea, but first I want to pray about it before I say anything more. Can you wait for my answer?"

90

Jessie laughed. "I'm not going anywhere soon, guess so."

"Thanks." Father left and headed down to the Chapel. Maybe I ought to go to the Atrium, since that is one of the spots that the budget is zeroing in on.

Jon did not remember ever saying anything directly to anyone about raising money for St. Elizabeth's Hospital, but everyone seemed to know that he was planning to do that. He shook his head in wonder when he considered how fast the gossip was spreading.

The interns waylaid him in the cafeteria and asked if it was true. Jon only laughed at them and said, "What if it is?"

The glint of life that shown in tired faces after a 24-hour shift encouraged him. Melody smiled and said that all she had heard was Father Jon was going to 'save' the hospital.

"That's a big order, even for a priest. And what if the hospital doesn't want to be saved?"

"Oh, Father," she grinned, "With you leading the campaign, who wouldn't want to be saved?"

"Now it is a campaign, is it?" He laughed some more.

When the Hospital Administrator stopped Jon in the hall, Jon began to take the rumors seriously. "I hear you have a plan to rescue St. Elizabeth's."

"I do?" Jon grinned. "It's a surprise to me."

"Who are you kidding, Father, you are the perfect one to bring in the funds. Everyone knows you or knows who you are."

"I'll let you know when plans develop. I won't do anything without the Bishop's blessing, including raising funds for here."

"Well, once you have you plans formulated, make an appointment with me. There are a few board members I'll have to placate. There seems to always be one or two elected every time that resist changes in how we do things. Don't suggest bingo around Molly as a fundraiser. She has it in mind that it is a form of gambling, and nothing will convince her otherwise.

"I'll keep that in mind," Jon noted.

"And Father, one of these days, stop by my office. I want to go to confession. I never seem to time it right to hit confession at St. Sophie's."

"I have time now," Father Jon replied. He knew what the next words were going to be.

"Oh, I am not spiritually prepared right now, but do come by some day and hear my confession."

"I will do that." Father Jon answered. He knew that the Administrator would never be 'spiritually prepared' at any time Jon was available. He worried about the man and prayed for him daily. The man was almost too glib in how he presented himself. He wondered about the family at home, and what kind of person the Administrator was with them.

When he got back to his apartment, he phoned the Bishop. The rumors were too active for him to wait any longer.

"Hello, Jon, I understand you are thinking about a fund drive for St. Elizabeth's."

"OK, Bishop, who told you that? I thought it was still all hidden away in my mind in the preplanning stages, and now we have all sorts of groups, including the interns, wanting to be part of 'my fund drive'. Even the Admin here stopped me and asked me how the plans were going."

The Bishop started laughing. "He is the one who called our office just a few minutes ago."

"Oh," was all Jon could think of saying. "He works fast. I just talked with him in the hall not more than twenty minutes ago, and he asked me about the plans then."

"Who is driving this idea, is that what you asked, Father Jon?"

"Yes, I know I am not - at least not yet."

"I am glad to hear that, for I would have thought you would have told me your ideas first."

"I was planning on that in this phone call, but the Admin beat me to the phone."

"Are you ready to talk about the ideas."

"No, Bishop, give me a day or two. If you hear of any such plans, you know that I am not behind them, yet. I will follow proper procedure, I assure you."

"I know you will, Father Jon."

The called ended with a blessing from the Bishop, who chuckled afterwards to himself. "Who is driving this, really?"

Jon found himself wrestling with the idea most of the night. Finally, he gave up near morning and left it the Lord's hands.

Jessie called early before his daily therapy. "Father, I thought you were going to come back and talk with me. The nurses say that you have started a fund raising campaign for the hospital. Wasn't that why you were asking me if I knew how to raise money?"

Jon looked at the phone incredulously. "Yes, Jessie, but I never told you anything, nor anyone else about it. Did you talk about it with any one?"

"No Father, I didn't. You told me to wait, and you would be back to talk with me."

"Think hard, Jessie, someone heard me speak with you and has made a huge mountain out of a mole hill. Got any ideas who?"

"No, Father, but I will think about it. Do you mean it is all a rumor?"

"At this point, yes."

"Gee, I am disappointed. I got excited when they told me. Was that wrong?"

"No, Jessie. What is wrong is that someone is trying to cause something to happen and using me as the prime candidate to make it happen."

Frankly, Jon was greatly irritated. He was short and abrupt with the therapist that morning. She was surprised with Jon's attitude.

Two days later, an excited Jessie called. "I think I know how the rumor got started!" She was almost shouting into the phone. "Will you visit me today?"

"I'll be up about eleven."

"You're not going to believe this when I tell you!"

"Oh, but yes, Jessie, I think I probably will." Jon hung up the phone. He was certain it started on Jessie's floor. Although he did not think Jessie had said anything, someone had overheard his brief conversation with her. He hoped Jessie knew who it was.

Later that week, Jon called Ramon and asked him to drive him to the Bishop's Office. Ramon was delighted to see his friend. "What are you doing with your time, Father?"

"Squelching rumors and planning to start one of my own."

"Oh, really," Ramon laughed. "Sounds interesting. Anything you can tell me about, or is it still all a secret?"

"If the Bishop approves, I'll tell you on the way home."

"And if the Bishop doesn't approve?" Ramon

94

asked.

"I'll work on the plan some more until I get his approval."

"This doesn't sound like the Father Jon I know who sticks his nose out and then receives the Bishop's blessing."

Jon laughed. "A bullet in the leg is a pretty tough chastisement from the Lord. I am not looking for another."

Ramon nodded, sobered by the memories.

The Bishop leaned back in his chair. "It sounds like a bee hive of intrigue there at St. Elizabeth's."

"Be that as it may, I am not the queen bee or in this case the 'king' bee," Father Jon replied.

"I appreciated the copies of the budget proposal that you sent up here. All three of those say different things. I've turned them over to the accountants and lawyers for analysis of the differences you noticed."

"I am not interested in the differences but in the proposed changes or deletions of jobs and services," Jon commented.

"I know, and that is where the rumors started, right?"

Jon nodded. "Here is a plan for fund raising that probably will work because it involves so many different aspects of the hospital, personnel, patients, and general public." He laid the fifty plus page plan on the Bishop's desk. "And on these two sheets is the abbreviated version of that document, basically for public knowledge."

The Bishop whistled. "You've been busy, and have a talent I didn't know about."

"No, your excellency, I have a fellow patient in the hospital who does this for a living. She knows the pit-falls and areas of caution."

"Who might this be, Father Jon?"

"Jessie, the young lady whose legs are repaired by the same surgeon as mine."

"Are you sure about her credentials?"

"Appendix A," Jon answered.

The Bishop flipped to the last pages of the fifty-plus and read. "She comes highly recommended, doesn't she? Is she volunteering her talent, or is she to be paid?"

"Under paid staff, she and the other person will receive a set stipend upon completion of the drive based on the total received but no more than the amount stated on the overall financial page. It is a small pittance compared to what she would be earning under other circumstances."

After flipping through the document, the Bishop found the financial page and nodded. "I see. I want to study this for several days before we announce this."

Jon's heart skipped in excitement. "Then you are thinking of letting us do that?"

"Of course, Jon. I know you, and you will give it everything you have to make it work. With Jessie's credentials and the other person named, I have no doubt this is a workable plan. I just want to make sure all legal loopholes are covered both for you and others who will make this work, the hospital and the Church. My part of the contribution, you might say."

"Thank you, Bishop. When?"

"Don't rush, my son." The Bishop moved slightly to one side. "Prayer is the first order of business, then analysis, then announcement and action. I have no doubt those tired interns and others there at the hospital want to get started, but we must make sure all the infrastructure is in place first."

96

Father Jon nodded. "So it is still a 'secret plan'?"

"That would be best for now. The rumor mill is really churning. Accidentally, or maybe with design, I suspect that this fund raising will reveal something we do not expect."

Jon raised his eyebrows. "Am I at the center of that? I thought I was just to be a Chaplain at the hospital. And now, of course, this fund raising."

"I don't think you are in any danger, Father. Would you rather not do this?" The Bishop held up the fifty plus pages.

Trying to keep calm, Jon discovered that fear had jumped into his spirit. "I think I need prayer, your Excellency."

"You're as white as your collar, Father. Are you all right?"

Biting his lower lip, Jon managed to nod. His breathing was shallow, and he felt faint. He had not remembered feeling such fear since the bullet struck his leg. He thought he must be getting old because fear had rarely visited him in his earlier years.

The Bishop was kneeling over him, praying. Jon wondered how he got on the floor. He started to sit up. "Just stay there, Father, for a few more minutes and breathe easy."

The Chancellor was beside the Bishop. "Shall I call 911?"

"No," the Bishop replied. "I think this is something the Lord is handling. Ramon is outside, isn't he?"

Ramon was ushered into the Bishop's office. His face paled when he saw Father Jon on the floor. A quick glance at the Bishop assured him that Jon was not ailing. What happened? He mouthed to his friend, the Bishop.

The Bishop had returned to his chair. "I think fear," he answered quietly.

Ramon's head popped up from where he was squatting beside Father Jon. "Fear?"

Father Jon was taking in the quiet conversation between his two friends, still in amazement that he was laying on the floor. Fear? How did the Bishop know? He hadn't said a word aloud, or had he? He struggled to sit up, with Ramon quick to lend a hand.

The Bishop asked, "Do you feel alright, Father?"

Father Jon nodded as he sat back down in the chair across from the Bishop. "What happened?"

"You asked for prayer, and down you went. Has this happened before?"

"No," Jon was chagrined. "I just felt fear like the fear I felt when I was shot. That is the closest thing I can think of."

"I thought so," answered the Bishop. "Did you ever have counseling after your injury?"

"No, they didn't seem to think I needed it. I guess I do. That," and Jon waved his hand towards the floor, "was an interesting reaction."

"Let's pray about this thing called 'fear' Father. You do know that there is a spirit of fear? I saw it in you one other time over in St. Ignatius, when your custodian acted like a caged wild animal. Do you remember?"

He did remember. It was like it had happened just that morning. "I prayed before the altar for sometime that morning, didn't I?"

"Yes, do you feel like you would like to do that again, now?"

"Now?" Jon echoed his Bishop's voice.
"Yes."

The three men retired to the Cathedral to

pray. Jon settled on his face before the high altar and wept as he prayed. He had not felt like such a small child in need of a daddy to pick him up and hold him in years. Ramon and the Bishop knelt several feet away and interceded for their friend.

Afterwards, the Bishop invited his two friends to dine with him. They enjoyed a close comradeship with each other.

"You seem very happy, Father," Melody's voice called out to him in the cafeteria. "Did you get the chance to ask about the fund raising?"

Father Jon looked at her. "Why do you ask that?"

"They say you went off campus from the hospital in an official car."

"Who are they?"

Melody blushed. "Rumor, oops."

"At least you have the conscience to blush." Jon sat down at the table with her. "I think there are a lot of people around here who need to close their mouths until an official word is given. That isn't criticism of you Melody, unless."

"Unless I am one who is gossiping, right?"

"Yes," Father's voice was soft and gentle.

"I'm sorry, Father. I guess I am guilty too. We are so eager to change the way things are that we grab onto anything that seems possible."

"And many things that are not true."

"That is true." Melody hadn't taken a bite out of her food since Father sat down.

"You need to eat." Jon reminded her.
She blushed again and nodded. "I needed what you said, too. Thanks."

"You're welcome." Father prayed over his food and began to eat. "Where are your buddies today?"

"Some are watching a surgery. I don't know where the others are. Fund raising?" There was a glint of humor in her eyes.

"Not that I know," Father Jon grinned.

Jessie looked up at her two visitors. Father Jon she knew, but who was the large heavy-set man with the bandages on his face and neck? He was wearing an expensive robe over what looked like leisure clothing.

"Jessie, this is the great tenor, Philippe La Costa. He is also a long term patient here in the hospital."

Jessie held out her hand in greeting. Philippe kissed her hand in the grand style of meeting royalty. "My pleasure, my lady. Father tells me you are a woman of great courage."

Jessie was speechless for just an instant. "It is so nice of you to call on me," she playacted back. "I do not carry a melody well, but we must get together sometime soon for tea." Then Jessie giggled.

Philippe rumbled his deep laugh.

Jon was biting his lip, something he seemed to do a lot lately, trying not to laugh until they did. "This should be fun." He was shaking his head. "You two sound like old timers instead of just meeting."

"Now that the introductions are finished," La Costa stated. "May I ask you to come visit me in my suite?"

Jessie's eyes got big. "Suite? Is that like a man asking a women up for a drink or to see his etchings?"

La Costa's laugh rumbled again. "Oh my lady, I would never do something like that."

Jessie blushed. "Father, put a stop to this!" She was laughing.

100

"I thought to keep prying ears from invading our talks that we would meet in Philippe's suite. Privacy is the rule in that section of the hospital. He thought meeting you in your room first would set you more at ease."

"I didn't think I could go off this wing," Jessie responded.

"I spoke with your doctor. If I take you, you can."

"What are we waiting for?" Jessie responded. "I am in my wheelchair for the next several hours."

"A woman of decision," Philippe chimed in. "I like that in my women."

"Now stop that!" Jessie blushed.

"Never fear, the good Father is your chaperon." Philippe smiled in spite of the bandages on his face.

Father Jon darted down the hall to the nursing station to inform them of where Jessie was going to be.

"Her doctor, your doctor, called and told us. I put a note on the face of her folder so that all the rest of the staff will know. She is going where?"

"Fifth floor, 553, Philippe La Costa is the patient there. They are getting acquainted down in her room right now."

"He is the big man with the neck and facial bandages? La Costa, is he that tenor?"

"Yes, autographs will come later," Jon said with a smile.

Jessie's eyes opened wide when she saw the plush fittings of the 5th floor. "This is in this hospital? Makes me feel like a pauper."

The pained look in Philippe's eyes told Father Jon that her remark had hurt. He wondered if it would interfere with the job of co-chairing the fund-raising events. He hoped not.

Once in the sitting room of Philippe's suite, with ice water to drink, Jon told them of the approval by the Bishop of the plan Jessie had put together. He had given Philippe a copy just the day before.

"Do you have an questions, Mr. La Costa?" Jessie asked as the professional fundraiser.

"Call me Philippe. No, I don't understand it all, but if the Bishop approves, I don't need to. Some things I sing I don't understand but they get acclaim from the audience." Philippe moved his chair so that they were seated around a small table. "You are the expert in this. Lead on Miss Jessie."

"Actually, Father is the leader, behind the scenes. We are the out front people. The ones they will photograph, talk to, interview, etc."

"Photograph? Philippe's hand went up to his bandages.

"Yes, we have already talked about that, Philippe," Father Jon added soothingly.

"Beauty and the beast!" Philippe seemed to choke on the words but then laughed. "Should be great publicity."

"We are not going to announce the fund raising until the 15th of next month. This should give us enough time to talk our way through together. Nothing is to be said outside of this room to anyone. Even if they ask what is going on!" Father Jon looked at each of them, and they nodded. "I am planning to work the so-called rumors so that they will be ripe for leadership on the 15th of next month. As spokespersons, you both should consider how you are going to handle the publicity and other chairman-type duties. You both are well known, first you Philippe, as a singer, and Jessie, because of the tremendous repair on your legs."

"You aren't exempted," Jessie reminded Jon.

102

"You are walking more and more without your cane. I saw the album Dr. Forbes has on your progress. It is impressive!"

"Point made," Jon acknowledged.

"So, we three patients are going to make a difference in this hospital," La Costa commended.

"With a lot of help from volunteers who will come out to assist one or the other of us in our cause," Jessie amended. "Without volunteers, this fund raising can not be done. A professional can only advise, he, she is only one person. Father, who is going to direct the volunteers?"

"I am still working on that. The Bishop has recommended several people. I have not talked to any one of them yet."

Later, in his apartment, Jon looked at the list the Bishop had given him and prayed. After an hour or so, he picked up the phone and called the Bishop. "Your Excellency, I have a problem. I can't seem to decide who on the list you gave me to call and ask about volunteering to direct the campaign here for the hospital."

A soft chuckle responded. "You are afraid of offending someone, right, Father Jon?"

"I suppose that is it. What if the one I call doesn't want to do the job and I have to call my second choice? Isn't that an insult to the second choice?"

Again the soft chuckle sounded in Jon's ears. The Bishop was shaking his head, which of course Jon could not see over the telephone. "My dear Father Jon, you are not normally without a decisive manner. If the second or third choice is offended, it is only because the first choice has failed to live up to her reputation as a leader. They would all rejoice in being asked. But I suppose I need to give you some guidance, which I thought I had with that list of five fine community leaders."

Father Jon was eager for someone else to make the decision, and it seemed the Bishop was with toying with his reluctance.

"Hasn't Jesus highlighted the one who will be the volunteer director?" The Bishop's voice had a smile in it. Jon shook his head 'no' at the phone before admitting he hadn't had such an enlightenment.

"In that case, call Edith Von Himmel."
Jon looked at the list. "Her name is not on this list!"

"I know, I thought of her after I made up that list. She will take the job and do a 'cracker jack' effort to recruit volunteers, get 'gobs' of publicity out and have a campaign that will definitely bring in the funds."

"She is of the Von Himmel Banking family, right?" Jon asked.

"Yes, and the best on the list, now that I have added her name to it. The others would each have been very capable, but Edith will bring in a certain vitality that the others can't."

"Thank you so much, Your Excellency. I was really at a lost, and the other two here at the hospital told me to get the job done. May I call her this evening, or would it be better to phone in the morning and go through the polite language that these people seem to expect when the less fortunate ones phone?"

A hearty laugh came over the telephone. "Call her at home this evening. She is expecting you to call. I took the liberty to ask her advice on this fund drive as an expert volunteer leader and discovered she was available and interested if you had not already gotten someone else."

After the Bishop had given him Edith Von Himmel's private phone number, Jon hung up the

104

phone and tore the original list in half before he call Mrs. Von Himmel.

"You have who?" Jessie asked the next day. "Edith Von Himmel." Jon smiled at the look on the young woman's face. "Why? Is she a bad choice?"

"People would kill to get her leadership or at least a promise of a gigantic donation. How did she respond when you asked her?"

"Graciously." Jon smiled. "She is coming here to the hospital to meet with you, La Costa and me this afternoon, unless you have some other engagement."

Jessie shivered in excitement. "But I don't have time to have my nails done or my hair set!"

Jon roared in laughter. "I don't think that will matter. She knows that all three of us are patients here."

"I know," Jessie giggled. "You see that, for a professional in my line of work, a name such as hers with her reputation is something we can usually only hope for once or twice in our careers. This is my first time doing this not as a 'gopher' for someone else, and Von Himmel is in my corner. Whee! I could almost jump up and dance!"

"You do that and you will have Dr. Forbes on you in an instant!" Jon smiled at Jessie's excitement.

Edith Von Himmel arrived at La Costa's suite with two large designer bags. Jessie and Jon arrived within minutes. Philippe arranged for a light snack to be delivered for this first meeting. As they four sat around the sitting room getting to know each other, Edith pulled from her bags matching dressy pullover tops. "I thought we might start with looking like we are serious about this fund raiser. I took the liberty to order these for each of you. One thing we do not want the community to think is that because you are in a hospital, you are relegated to hospital gowns that tie up the back."

"Ma'm," La Costa spoke up. "May I share in the costs of these shirts? It would seem unfair to have you foot the bill."

Edith laughed. "Philippe, I would be delighted to share the cost. And, also, you may address me as Ms. Von Himmel. Ma'm sort of makes me feel older than I am." Philippe nodded his head.

Jon felt the smooth luxurious texture of the fabric. "I will have to choose the times I wear my shirt, you understand, Ms. Von Himmel."

"Of course, Father, but there will be times when the more casual look will be appropriate, even for you." Edith smiled. "I will speak with the Bishop if that is a concern."

"Oh no, I just will have to pick my times carefully." Jon laughed.

Jessie pulled her shirt over her head before picking up her notebook. "As the professional, I have some ground rules we need to go over, and then I would like your input, Ms. Von Himmel, as to what you are comfortable with in leadership."

For several hours, the four discussed and remapped the initial fund raising program. Edith was excited about directing volunteers to raise money for all the needy areas of the hospital. Jessie cautioned about the need for a preset formula for distribution of the funds in the unlikelihood that the over all goal would not be met.

They agreed to meet two days later. "What do you think?" Jessie asked Father Jon as he pushed her back to her room.

"I am glad you are directing this and Edith is willing to shoulder such a big burden as coordinating the volunteers." Jessie was still wearing her new shirt. They had reached the main floor.

"Want a chocolate milkshake before going back to your room?"

Jessie nodded then said, "Only, I didn't bring any money with me."

"I didn't ask if you had, I asked if you wanted one." Father Jon turned into the Wayside Snack Bar and parked Jessie by a table. "Back in a moment."

This was the first time Jessie had been in the Wayside, although occasionally someone brought her milkshakes from the snack bar. She noticed several other patients enjoying being away from their regular floors and reading her shirt. Jon put the two milk shakes on the table and straightened Jessie's chair so she could comfortably reach it.

"Sort of different for me, to be adjusting another's chair and not having to have someone adjust mine." Father Jon took a big slurp from his shake. "It is about time you got to go somewhere besides up and down that hall your room is on."

"I was noticing how strange it feels." Jessie was looking around. "I guess I will have to come here more often if I can get my escort to bring me. I like this." Jessie was holding up her shake.

"Are the first meetings as confusing as the one we just had upstairs, Jessie?"

"Things don't start to make sense until about the third or fourth meeting. By that time, we all get a sense of the goal, the same goal, and our individual job descriptions begin to make sense." Jessie frowned a little. "I thought it just was due to the professional over me directing it that way until he showed me that it took that much time to get to the purpose, and goal settled well in the leadership's collective mind."

Jon threw their trash away. "Upstairs,

Cinderella. They will send a posse out looking for you if I don't get you back soon. We are past the hour when I said we would be back."

"Father, Father," the soft voice of Sister Margaret Louise called out to them as they entered the main corridor. She came scurrying up as fast as she could push her walker in front of her. "I thought something had happened to Jessie. I see that I am wrong."

Jessie smiled at the petite nun. "I was having an outing, and we stayed out beyond curfew. Sorry to have worried you, Sister."

Sister Margaret Louise chuckled. "Wait until the rumors get around that you were out with the good Father. What is this hospital getting to be? A dating place?" Sister had now folded her walker and hooked it over the back handles of Jessie's chair. "I will see that she gets back, Father Jon. They have been paging you from Administration after the story got out that you were meeting with Edith Von Himmel. Two dates in one afternoon! Really, Father!"

Father Jon looked down at his pager. "Oops, I guess we were having so much fun, Jessie, that I forgot to turn this thing back on." Jon grinned. "Since you are now in such capable hands, I'll catch up with the Administration pronto."

Jessie scowled. "If it is about our meeting, isn't the Admin being premature?"

"Yes but no. He has a way of starting rumors and doesn't like to get his information through the normal channels. I'll go to see him and call you later if there is anything you need to know."

"Father Jon, call me either way. I am uncomfortable with the idea of him spreading rumors before we are ready to announce this thing." Jessie smiled slightly.

108

Jon nodded and watched Sister Margaret Louise push Jessie to the nearest elevator.

"Going my way?" A familiar voice interrupted Jon's thoughts. He turned almost too quickly and found himself in the embrace of Ramon.

"Watch it, Jon, you could take a spill turning that quickly." Ramon gently steered Jon to a nearby seat.

"What are you doing here?" Jon took in the hospital security uniform Ramon was wearing.

"Working." Ramon's eyes laughed. "It seems we are teamed up together again."

"Why?" Jon asked softly.

"The Bishop, why else?" Ramon again laughed softly. "He thought it prudent to get me hired here. What are his reasons? I don't know. He phoned yesterday and told me that I was to report to Hospital Security today. So here I am."

Jon's head was swimming. "Well, I am glad to see you and have you here. However, I don't like the deep uneasiness I feel knowing the Bishop has made this arrangement. Makes me wonder what else he knows that is going on that warrants 'protection' by you."

"Maybe I am just an available prayer partner."

"For what it is worth, the Administrator has been paging me all afternoon, and I turned my pager off while I was in a meeting with Edith Von Himmel, Philippe La Costa and Jessie in Philippe's suite."

"So I'll walk you over to the East Wing. The way you staggered when you turned tells me you are pretty tired. Want a wheelchair ride?"

"No!" Jon snapped. "But, a steady hand at my elbow will be appreciated." Jon rose slowly from the chair. The pager at his belt sounded it's alert. Jon looked down. "We'll stop at the first house

109

phone, and I will call in my apology for the delay in answering this thing! Maybe then I will find out why he has been paging me since just about the time Edith got here."

The secretary in the Administration Office voiced regrets as she told Father Jon that the Admin had left for the afternoon. "Anything special you need from him?" she asked sweetly.

If Ramon hadn't been at his elbow, Jon might have just sat down in bewilderment. "I have multiple pages on my pager from the Admin this afternoon. I was tied up in a meeting and unable to respond. Please leave a message that I did return his page as soon as I was able. Thank you." Jon hung up the phone.

Ramon gently steered him toward his apartment. "A mystery?" he asked.

Once inside the small apartment and in his recliner, Jon faced his friend. "That doesn't make any sense."

Ramon chuckled. "Maybe this is why I am here."

For the rest of the afternoon, Jon and Ramon talked. Ramon had been on his way out of the hospital when he had chanced to see Father Jon, Sister Margaret Louise, and Jessie in the hall.

"Chance never seems to be the reason we meet up," Jon mentioned dryly.

"Do you remember those cement patches in the church and rectory basements?" Ramon asked. Jon nodded. They were excavated by the police department and found to contain jewelry missing for at least thirty years. Apparently a clever thief thought the church and rectory would be a safe storage space."

"Jewelry?" Jon shook his head. "Was it stolen from stores or private collections?"

110

"That is the interesting part. It did come from private collections. Several wealthy families who used to attend St. Ignatius years ago owned the jewelry. The police are still trying to piece together who had access to the church and rectory basement at the time the jewelry came up missing. It does seem to point to someone who was familiar with each and all the families, and that person is dead now."

"So the families will get the jewelry back?"

"Most of it, as it was not insured like they do nowadays. Some will go to the insurance companies who did pay off on the stolen goods years and years ago."

"Their worth has increased, I imagine."

"Sure has. Now are you ready for the unusual twist, Father?"

"As long as I don't have to do anything about it." Jon laughed. "You look like you can hardly wait to tell me!"

"Vincent Sardoni knew about the buried treasure. And he wanted it, which is why he was trying so hard to push the Catholic Church into abandoning the site."

"Vincent? Was he the thief?"

"No, from what they can piece together, one of those many hoodlums that passed through Vincent's shifty organization in the early years was the original thief. Probably got careless and bragged about the jewels. He was one of the early disappearances in Sardoni's career."

Jon laughed. "You're not just leading me on, are you, Ramon? That story is about as fantastic as the one I actually lived at St. Ignatius."

"I'll get you the documentation. The Bishop has a full copy. It is fascinating reading."

The next morning, Jon was about half way through shaving when the phone rang. Jon grabbed if up on the fifth ring. "Father Jon."

Jessie was crying. "Can you come up here?"

"Yes. What is wrong?"

"Just come, Father, and soon." The telephone line went dead.

Jon finished the obvious part on his face and pulled on a cleric shirt. He reached for his pocket size bottles of oil and Holy Water.

"Father, Father, the Administrator is looking for you." One of the girls in the accounting office called out when he went by the Business Office. He nodded and waved and kept on heading for the elevator.

He got off the on Jessie's floor and headed for her room. "You can't go in there now, Father," the nurse called to him as he went by. Even though the door was shut, he could hear voices inside Jessie's room. After his authoritative knock, Jon barely waited for a response before he opened the door.

"Glad to see you, Father." Dr. Forbes was standing at Jessie's bed. "She has gone into a deep sleep now. I induced it. She was in the most pain I have ever seen her in."

Father Jon went to the other side of Jessie's bed and looked down at her. She showed no recognition when he spoke to her. He prayed over her and anointed her with oil.

Dr. Forbes was entering data on the portable computer terminal that had been pushed into Jessie's room. "I don't like this reaction at all," he muttered to himself. "I have ordered x-rays and echo grams of both legs. I probably will uncover her legs in surgery later this morning. Do a pre-op prep," he told the attending nurse.

Father Jon followed Dr. Forbes out of the room. "She was up in a wheelchair for several hours

112

yesterday afternoon. Would that have set this all off?"

"No."

"What about a chocolate milkshake?"

Dr. Forbes looked up at Father Jon.

"She had one late yesterday afternoon."

The doctor smiled slightly. "I almost thought you were asking me if I wanted one."

Jon laughed.

"Doctor, I have just read through the night shift's report," a voice slightly muffled behind a computer monitor spoke. "Jessie requested extra medication eleven times during the night. It is recorded that the Pain-No pump measured out the proper dosage on the monitor. However, when I came on this morning the pump vial was still full! And there is no record that the vial was replaced. Let me check the locked cabinet."

"Sit down, Father Jon. You look like you had a rough night also." Dr. Forbes was proud of his patient and didn't want Jon to over-tire himself.

"Actually, I slept all night. Jessie's SOS by phone was the first of the day."

"How are the plans coming for the fund raiser? Are you still going to have it?" The doctor looked over at the nurse when she reappeared behind the desk.

"All drugs accounted for, so that vial hasn't been changed."

"Let's take another look at Jessie and check that IV insert." The nurse and doctor disappeared into Jessie's room. A few minutes later, they returned. "Mystery solved. It was a block in the tube running to Jessie. Poor girl, she wasn't getting anything whenever she pressed the button."

Dr. Forbes was scowling at the data terminal. "But it was reading out here that she was. Get a new pump on her pronto! I don't want that happening again. She has enough to handle without a faulty Pain-No drip."

"The fund raiser, doctor? Yes it is on. We met with the volunteer chairman yesterday. Do you know Edith Von Himmel?"

"The Edith Von Himmel? Banking and stock brokerage Von Himmel?"

"I don't imagine there are two of them in this town," Jon replied.

"Impressive." The doctor was typing something into the computer. "With her expertise and name recognition, the fund drive should go very well."

"We certainly hope so. It is still over a month away from the start of the drive. Jessie and Edith were like two peas in a pod talking about all the needs to make the fund drive a success yesterday. Having her," Jon nodded toward Jessie's room, "incapacitated even for a few days will slow things down."

The doctor stood as he logged out of the computer. "It will be a success, Father Jon. There are a lot of people who are counting on it and willing to roll up their shirt sleeves, so to speak, to make it work." He patted Jon on the shoulder. "Jessie should wake up in about four hours, and hopefully the Pain-No pump will do its job this time."

Doctor Forbes was down the hall and around the corner before Father Jon could think of a response. The nurse smiled. "Go finish your shaving. I'll call you when she is awake again."

"It shows, huh?" he asked.

"Yep."

Jon had just exited the elevator when his pager went off. Glancing down at the glowing green screen, Jon grimaced, the Admin again. "No shave yet," he muttered as his steps took him to the hospital administration office door.

The secretary was just ready to key in a second page to Jon as he stepped through the doorway. "Oh, you are here!" the flustered girl said with a start. At the same moment, the Administrator's loud voice called to her over the intercom, demanding that she page Jon again.

"He is not in a very good mood," she said softly as she looked up, embarrassed at the tone and choice of vulgar words that Jon had also just heard.

"Not your fault," Jon responded grimly. "What is his problem?"

The woman had her hand over the mouthpiece of the phone. She mouthed 'alcohol and a disagreement with his wife'.

Jon nodded and stepped over to the closed office door and raised his hand to knock. The secretary connected with the Administrator's phone. "Father Jon is here, sir."

Jon tapped on the door and swung it open to reveal a red-faced man. Jon wondered briefly whether the ruddy complexion was from drink or anger or both.

Closing the door behind him, Father Jon approached the ranting man sitting behind the massive executive desk. He noted the general disarray and clutter on the desk, including a nearly empty glass with a hint of amber fluid at the bottom. The words that flowed out that drunken, angry man's mouth were words Father Jon normally did not hear. He pulled a chair up close to the desk and prayed for wisdom as he listened. Finally, the tirade of angry vulgar words stopped as the administrator ran out of steam.

Jon reached for his pager.

"Who gave you the right to talk with Mrs.

Von Himmel about the hospital's financial affairs!" It wasn't a question but a statement. "She and her husband are major financial backers of this hospital and do not want this information to be public. Everybody and his brother would started begging off of them if this information gets out."

Father Jon did not say anything.

"Answer me!" shouted the angry man.

"The Bishop."

"The Bishop! How did he get into this?"

"Saint Elizabeth's is under his care in this diocese, isn't it?"

"Meddling! That is what you are doing! Meddling with something that you know nothing about."

"I am appointed a Chaplain here by the diocese." Jon answered in a soft voice.

"You are nothing more than a glorified patient! What's more, you can vacate that 'suite' and get back into a regular hospital bed until your doctor dismisses you." Then the man sat there and wept.

Jon's mind was running full tilt, trying to figure out what was the matter with the administrator. He realized the consumption of a considerable amount of alcohol played part of the role. The office smelled like a brewery. It was obvious that, even to his untrained medical eye, the administrator was in serious trouble. As a pastor-priest, he knew that although he could not tell anything, it was going to be necessary to get the man help soon.

"Ed," Father Jon decided to use the man's first name. "Would you like to pray together? You have said in the past that you would like me to hear your confession. Maybe now is a good time."

"No," Ed sobbed out. "God isn't interested in me."

116

Relieved that Ed was no longer bellowing at him, Jon punched the Security button on his pager and hoped that Ramon was on duty. When the green screen glowed, Jon was relieved to see it was Ramon's code answering. He turned the microphone on and said softly, "Come quickly, Admin Office."

There was no indication that Ed even was aware Jon had spoken. The man was sobbing incoherently.

Jon stepped over to the closed door and opened it a crack. Inquisitively, the secretary looked up. Jon just put his finger to his lips and nodded toward the outer door. Running steps could be heard in the hallway. Ramon burst into the outer office, followed by another security officer.

"In here," Jon quickly beckoned.

Ramon turned and told the second officer to wait with the secretary before he entered the Administration Office with Jon. His experienced eye took in everything immediately. "Oh, God," he blurted out.

"Who's you?" Ed looked up, his face a mess from crying. "Leave me alone!" Then the drunken man vomited all over himself and the massive desk.

Ramon pulled out his radio. "ER, send up your best to the Administration office. A gurney, a mop up crew and a doctor."

"Can we keep this from circulating in the hospital?" The executive secretary was standing in the door.

Ramon nodded. "Larry," he said to his partner. "Close off this wing and require all staff in the offices to stay put until we notify them otherwise."

Larry nodded and stepped out into the hall to secure the area.

Jon was now at the side of the very ill man,

holding the man's head tenderly against his chest, attempting to keep the man from wallowing in his own vomit. Ramon moved the massive desk with one violent shove and pulled the ill man's chair away from it. He looked into Jon's face and saw tears streaming down it. Ramon grunted as he maneuvered the now incoherent man in the executive office chair further into the open room. Two orderlies pushing a gurney, and an ER doctor came charging into the office.

It wasn't difficult for the doctor to tell what was the matter with the ill Administrator. Despite the prevailing vomit odor, the smell of alcohol was very evident. Jon loosened his hold on the man as the orderlies expertly transferred him to the gurney. The doctor inquired of Father Jon, "Did you find him this way?" Jon just nodded. The orderlies tossed Father Jon some throwaway scrub cloths as they readied to wheel Ed out of his office. "Better phone his wife," the doctor said as he steadied the gurney through the door.

The executive secretary was already on the phone. She gave a weak smile and nod to the doctor. After giving instructions to his fellow security officers, Ramon accompanied the very grieved priest to his suite. Jon pulling his wet, stained, and putrid clothing off and thrust them into a trash bag Ramon had picked up as they passed the janitorial closet.

It took Jessie a couple of days to recover from her night with the faulty pump. Edith Von Himmel stopped in to visit with Jessie and assured her that the excellent planning Jessie had already done gave her enough to work with until Jessie was again able to participate. In that intervening time period, Father Jon and Philippe La Costa were photographed in various parts of the hospital as Edith Von Himmel directed.

The Assistant Administrator took over the running of the hospital. Father Jon and he agreed to keep information about the ill Administrator confidential until it was determined if his alcoholism would disqualify him from his job. Ramon, on his first day off from Security, took Jon to visit with the Bishop. Both Edith Von Himmel and the Bishop assured Father Jon that there was no secrecy in the Von Himmel donations to Saint Elizabeth's. Edith pointed out the contribution dedication plaque in the wing where Ed was now hospitalized. "Poetic justice," Ramon murmured when Jon showed it to him.

Jon responded, "Or maybe Godly preparation for his day of need."

The Saint Elizabeth's Fund Drive kicked open with a massive picnic and carnival for the city one bright sunny Saturday. Edith arranged for a black tie fund raising dinner by 'invitation only' the Friday night before the fund drive picnic. Jessie was ecstatic with the turn out. The 'three stooges,' as they called themselves were guests of honor, along with key personnel of the hospital who were responsible for particular areas being targeted in the fund drive. Dr. Forbes declined to be present, stating that since Jessie and Father Jon were there, they were evidence of what his work would accomplish.

In spite of all of the positive activities, Father Jon was discontented. He spent more and more time alone, sometimes in his room and, at other times, in the chapel. Sister Margaret Louise was not tolerating the treatment for her cancer, and she found it difficult to go to Jessie's room very often. Jessie mentioned the elderly sister's absences to Jon, but he didn't seem to hear her concern.

Philippe La Costa's wife paid an unexpected

visit to the hospital and ridiculed his involvement with the fund drive. "You singing senile fool!" Her parting remark sent him to bed in a deep depression.

The interns that Melody often was with were more and more stressed out by the end of their year of internship. The one who had been so discontent earlier in the year took a long weekend off and failed to return. He just seemed to drop out of existence. Melody was especially concerned about his well being and tried to talk with Father Jon about it. Father seemed to be listening to what she was saying, but he gave her little comfort or advice.

Ramon grew increasingly more concerned about Father Jon. He remembered the weeks after the fires around St. Ignatius when Jon had been in such grief. Ramon spent many hours trying to remember what pulled Jon out of that time of depression.

One day, he got a phone call from his friend, the Bishop. "Do you see much of Father Jon?" he asked.

"Less than I used to," replied Ramon.

"Something is wrong," replied the Bishop. "Find out what it is."

"Well, it is not the fund drive," Ramon answered.

"I agree. Edith is doing a phenomenal job, along with that young lady, Jessie."

"They are going to be way over goal."

"A rare thing these days. They are talking about investing the excess for the needy in the future." The Bishop chuckled. "Jon ought to be really happy over that."

"I don't think Jon even knows." Ramon responded and frowned. "This reminds me of the time after the fires. You do remember that, Your Excellency?"

120

"Yes," was the Bishop's sober reply. "What was the remedy at that time? Do you recall, Ramon?"

"The boys prayed for him, and Father Marvin requested he concelebrate Mass with him."

The Bishop was silent. "Are you still there, Your Excellency?"

"Yes, I am thinking. I will phone you back later. I have an idea."

"Can you get hold of the boys? Maybe Father Jon needs to remember also."

"I think I can. They still hang around St. Ignatius or Rudy White's church most of the time."

Ramon was whistling when he left duty that afternoon. He looked for Father Jon before he left and even phoned his room. He thought about paging him but decided that would be his action the following day if he couldn't readily locate the good Father. In the meantime, he was going to enlist the help of the gang.

Jon was sitting moodily in the hospital chapel. He had just talked with a family torn by grief at the senseless death of a small child. Somehow, the things they shared fed the emptiness that Jon felt. He heard a familiar plinking of the soft rubber tips on the legs of a walker. He thought it odd that even a walker had an individualist sound that enabled a person to know who was propelling the object. It was the same as identifying footsteps. The chapel door swung open as the walker clattered against it.

"There you are, Father," a meek voice penetrated the silence of the chapel.

Jon looked up from his self-imposed sorrow and depression. "Sister Margaret Louise," he greeted her.

"I've been looking all over for you," the petite nun said.

"I haven't been hiding," Jon answered what he felt was an accusation.

"Oh dear! I know that!" hastily answered the aged nun. "But you haven't been answering your pages either."

Jon reached into his pocket for the pager. "I guess I have had it turned off." He looked at the pager screen after he turned it on. "This thing is a nuisance anyway," he said as he turned it back off.

The eighty-plus year old sister now was seated on a bench of the chapel. "Where are all the things that should be in this chapel?"

Jon tossed his head toward the locked closet in the corner. "In there. It seems that religious objects are disturbing to some who drop in here." His voice dripped with sarcasm. The elderly nun raised her eyes, first in astonishment at Father's comment. Then her eyes snapped in indignation at Father's attitude displayed by his sarcastic tone.

"Why Father!" her voice pitch raised. Then she placed her hand over her mouth for daring to speak out with that voice tone to a priest.

Jon ignored her rebuke as he angrily voiced his disgust with the hospital administration. "Notice that there is nothing in this room to offend anybody! There is nothing to indicate that the Catholic Church has anything to do with this place. Totally secular! Nothing more than a room set aside where people can come to be alone when life overwhelms them with sickness and death!"

"Can't you do something about it?" Sister Margaret Louise said softly. "You are a chaplain here."

"So are a couple of dozen other people, chaplains that is."

Margaret Louise decided not to respond but turned her heart and mind to praying in this isolated

122

and ignored room. It had always been a chapel in her mind and, even with the obvious trappings missing, the presence of God still seemed to be in the room.

Jon listened to the elderly woman softly prayed the Way of the Cross. He joined his voice with hers. Step by step, the two of them moved their eyes from one spot to the next as though the objects had not been removed from the walls some months earlier. As Sister Margaret Louise began to tire, Father Jon continued on as her voice becoming less audible.

"You are tired, Sister. Do you want me to stop?"

The elderly lady shook her head 'no', "You finish, I'll listen," she whispered.

Later, Jon found a stray wheelchair in the hall and pushed the nun back to her room. "Will you stay a little while?" Sister asked as the nurse's aides came into the room to put her into bed.

"Come back in ten to fifteen minutes, Father," one aide said.

Promising to return when they had Sister in bed, Jon went out to the nursing station. "We are glad you brought her up," said a nurse. "She had told us she was going to see you when she left, and we were not sure where she was."

Jon slumped down on a vacant stool to wait. "You know she is going back to the convent tomorrow to live?" Another nurse spoke up.

Jon's head jerked up. "What?"

"She didn't tell you? I thought that was why she went downstairs to see you."

Father Jon was speechless. The nurse continued, "Her doctor doesn't see any reason for her to remain here. She has finished all the treatment for her cancer that the doctor feels is useful."

"Does Jessie know?" Father Jon's mind

slowly was grabbing at reasons that Sister would remain in the hospital.

"Yes, they talked together a long time earlier today, and I might add, cried together. That young woman is really special for Sister Margaret Louise. I think she is the reason Sister agreed to try the therapy for her cancer."

"She has been a mainstay for Jessie," Jon murmured.

"And lately, Jessie has been a big help and comfort for Sister."

"Why didn't someone tell me?" Jon asked softly.

"She told us not to tell anybody, especially you." The nurse smiled. "She wanted to tell you herself."

"So I guess I'll have to go on pretending I don't know." The nurses nodded.

"Sister is ready for you, Father," the pert aide said as she arrived at the nursing station.

Jon nodded solemnly and stood up and stretched. "Good luck," one nurse smiled at him.

Sister Margaret Louise was waiting on him. "Turn that top light off, Father. The young ladies seemed to have forgotten it in their leaving."

"You wanted to talk with me?" Jon sat in the chair indicated by Sister close beside her.

"I am leaving here tomorrow," she whispered. Her bright eyes searched Father Jon's face. "Did you know that my cancer is not responding to treatment?"

Jon reached out his hand and took hers. "The nurses told me while the others got you ready for bed. How long have you known?"

"About a week," she said softly. "They have arranged for my care over in the convent. There is a room set up for me on the first floor. The Sisters will

124

care for me until I go home."

"It isn't very long, is it?" Jon was feeling a stab of grief in his spirit.

"No, just a few days, a week or so." Margaret Louise's face glowed. "A short time until I am with my Savior and Lord." A trace of a smile was on her face.

"Do you want communion tonight?"

"Yes, Father, after . . ."

A nurse interrupted when she entered the room. "Oh, excuse me. I didn't realize anyone was in here with you, Sister Margaret Louise. I need to get your temperature and listen to your heart. Can you excuse us moment?"

Jon stood. "I will go get the elements and will return in a few minutes, Sister Margaret Louise."

After a barely perceptible nod, the nun turned her eyes to the nurse bustling about. "You are new tonight, aren't you?"

"Yes'm."

"Did you know it really doesn't matter much about my pulse or temperature? I am dying."

"You don't know that!" snapped the nurse.

"If you read my chart, you would know that. And you would also know a dying person is entitled to privacy with a priest."

"He's a priest? He doesn't look like one." The nurse was now holding Sister's wrist and scowling at her watch. "Now, I'm done. Shall I turn out your light?"

"No," Sister Margaret Louise said, almost with a tone of irritation. "Father is coming back to give me communion."

"He is going to visit this late in the evening?" The nurse finished tucking the sheet and blanket snuggly around the petite nun. Snapping off the light, she turned and left the room without waiting on an answer to her last question.

A light tap on the door announced the return of Father Jon. "I see she left you in the dark." He turned on the low lamp on the side table.

"You'd better hang a DO NOT DISTURB sign on the door, Father."

"I spoke to her at the desk. Cheery one, isn't she?"

"I shall pray for her during the night, Father."

Once back in his own rooms, Jon sat in the dark just thinking. The little light on his telephone was blinking. Wearily, he punched the play button. "You have seven messages," the mechanical voice stated. Jon hoped none would require him to go back out into the hospital as chaplain. There were two quietly spoken messages from Sister Margaret Louise, and a quick one from Ramon. The last message was from Jessie. He punched repeat to listen to it again.

"Father Jon, this is Jessie. Can you meet us in Sister Margaret Louise's room at six in the morning? She told me that by the time you get this message that you will know she is moving back to the convent. Don't be late. We are trying to beat the early morning hallway traffic. See you then, Father!"

There were other voices quietly speaking in the background during Jessie's message. Jon wasn't sure whose voices they were. He puzzled over the message for a few more minutes before glancing at the hands on his clock. Six in the morning would come around fast, so he hurried with his nightly routine and sank down onto his bed. Suddenly, he sat up again and set his alarm before falling back and was asleep instantly.

There were overlapping shifts of nurses on duty as Jon made his way to Sister Margaret Louise's room. They barely looked up as Jon came down the

126

hallway. From the Visitors Lounge for that hallway, Jessie beckoned to Father Jon. Philippe La Costa was there, decked out in a splendid robe. "We are waiting on Edith Von Himmel," Jessie said by way of information.

"This early in the morning?" Jon's eyebrows lifted. "What is going on?"

"Human interest publicity," the cultured voice of Edith spoke behind him. Edith, as well dressed as usual, stood in the lounge doorway. A neatly dressed gentleman stood just behind her. "This is Mark Wilte, the columnist. Jessie, Father Jon, and Philippe La Costa."

The three acknowledged the introduction. "We left the photographer downstairs cooling his heels," Edith smiled. "Mark can write the story without the readers having invaded Sister Margaret Louise's privacy with a photograph."

"This early morning gathering, does she know about it?" asked Jon, somewhat perplexed and feeling uninformed.

"Yes," Jessie answered quietly. "She agreed to let Philippe sing a song to her as his tribute to the woman who nursed you and me through those first few weeks after our legs were repaired."

"And you have arranged it so the story will be told to the whole city?"

"Discreetly, I assure you, Father." The 'golden tongue' columnist said quietly.

Edith smiled. "The Von Himmel family has a strong interest in the paper."

"Of course," said Jon. "And the Catholic Church also?"

"Meaning?" Edith inquired.

"As a representative of the church, I can not allow Sister Margaret Louise to be exploited."

"She isn't, I assure you," responded Mark

Wilte. "This is a powerful human interest story. It has a direct impact on the making of the hospital a little more user friendly."

Father Jon still felt a little cautious about being a part of this event.

"As you always say, Father, let's pray together before we go to Sister's room." Jessie smiled. "Sister was fine with this when I discussed it with her."

"Did she know a reporter would be present?" Jon looked first to Jessie, then Edith and Mark.

"Yes," Edith answered. "I asked her if that was all right with her after Jessie had mentioned about a reporter."

"What was her answer?" Jon queried.

"She said 'yes', Father."

"Then let's pray and get this tribute on its way."

Several nurses looked up from their early morning briefing and smiled as the small group made its way to Sister Margaret Louise's room.

Sister was awake and waiting. She tried to make them all comfortable with her leaving the hospital. Philippe La Costa stepped up to her side, gently took her frail hand into his, and began to sing. *Panis Angelicus*. How appropriate Jon thought, *Bread of Angels.*

When La Costa finished singing, he looked down into the sweet face of Sister smiling at him. "You know, dear lady, that your angelic ministrations to these two dear friends of mine has touched my heart and soul with a depth of love I never have known before. Thank you for being here for them." A nurse standing in the doorway was crying. All of them in the room seemed to have glistening eyes. Jon wondered why he had been opposed to this gathering just a few minutes before.

128

Edith Von Himmel and Mark Wilte slipped out of the room first. "Beautiful," Mark murmured.

"Touchingly holy," Edith agreed.

In the evening paper, Mark's column told of the almost angelic event that took place that morning as fellow patients honored the leaving of a dear friend.

After giving Sister Margaret Louise one final blessing, Jon went down to physical therapy to see if there was an early cancellation and he could get his therapy early. "You are in luck, Father, there have been two this morning."

"I don't think I could handle a double session," laughed Jon. "But I could use a nap."

"Up early?" the therapist put Jon through his exercises.

"You can read about it in the paper." Jon grinned. "I'm not going to give the story away."

"Maybe I ought to keep you for a double session and 'sweat' it out of you."

"I'll tell Doc Forbes on you," Jon retorted. Later, resting on his bed, Jon thought about the courageous nun and the equally courageous tenor upstairs and the little gal by the name of Jessie. His life was touched by really interesting people.

Early the next morning, the phone rang. Jon was tempted to let the message go on to the answering machine. After a nudge from his conscience, Jon rolled over to the edge of the bed to answer it. "Father Jon."

The caller was the Bishop. Jon sat up instantly alert. "I will be celebrating the Requiem Mass at the convent across the street from the hospital this afternoon. Sister Margaret Louise went home during the night."

"She is gone already?" Jon was trying to make his brain catch up with the voice on the

129

telephone.

"Yes, she timed it close, but she died 'at home' as she wanted. They will bury her late this afternoon in their cemetery behind the wall."

"Private, of course," Jon murmured.

"Yes, but Mother Superior did say that you and that young lady and the tenor would be welcome to attend the celebration Mass in the Chapel. That is a private invitation, you do understand. There will be seats reserved there for your convenience."

"That is highly irregular, isn't it, Your Excellency?"

"I approved," the Bishop said quietly.
Jon made quick work with his morning toilet and headed out to Jessie's room.

"Morning, Father, you are out early." One of the nurses looked up from what she was doing at the nursing station.

"Is Jessie awake?"

"Do you want me to check, Father?"

"Yes, please." Jon stood outside Jessie's room door while the nurse went inside.

"She is awake. You may go in."
Jon hesitated in the doorway before he went fully into the room.

Jessie studied his serious countenance as she looked up from what she was reading. "Something is wrong, Father?"

Jon pulled up a chair beside her bed. Licking his lips pensively, he asked, "What are you reading?"

"Something Sister gave to me. She asked that I read it everyday. I don't understand everything, but she said after awhile God would enlighten my mind and heart, and I would understand."

Looking down, Jon hesitated a moment. "Jessie, Sister went home as a bride last night."

"She died?"

130

He nodded.

Jessie lay back on her bed. "Oh." Her voice was nearly inaudible. "Do you think she knew when she left here yesterday?"

"More than likely she knew the time was near." Jon answered humbly.

Jessie cried softly for a few minutes as Father Jon prayed and allowed her a few moments of grief.

"There is more."

Jessie wiped her tears and looked expectantly toward Father. "Not another death?" she asked.

"No, we are invited to the funeral Mass in the Chapel at the Covent. You and I and Philippe, that is."

"Oh," whispered the young woman.

"The main part will be behind the 'grill' that separates the public from the cloistered sisters. It is highly irregular to have any outsiders attend. The Bishop will be the Celebrant. Sister Margaret Louise asked that we might attend, and the Bishop has given his permission."

"When will it be?"

"Later this afternoon." Jon looked at Jessie. "Do you want to attend?"

"Oh yes," Jessie's eyes sparkled. "But is it wheelchair accessible?"

"Good question. I will find out and the exact time when we need to be there. Now I must go up and see Philippe La Costa."

Father took his leave as Jessie lay there thinking about the courageous woman they had just honored the day before. It was hard to imagine the petite nun gone.

Philippe was stirring when Jon got to his room. "What?" he blustered when he saw Father so early in the morning.

"Sit down, Philippe. I need to share some

news with you."

"I was just getting ready to have some breakfast, Father. Have you eaten already?"

"No," Father said as he accepted the cup of tea Philippe offered him.

"Make yourself comfortable then. They always send me enough for two. I guess they think because of my size, I need more." Then the rumbling laugh that often accented Philippe's conversation spilled forth.

"I have a special request for you from Sister Margaret Louise," Jon began hesitantly.

Philippe's face changed to one of compassion. "Anything that dear lady wants, if it is within my power, she can have."

"She wants you to attend her funeral Mass this afternoon in the Chapel at the Convent with Jessie and me."

La Costa's face contorted as he tried to make sense of what Father Jon just told him. "She passed already? Oh My God!" Philippe covered his face with his massive hands. His sob sounded as a deep groan as he slumped down in his chair. "Of course, I will. Does 'little' Jessie know?"

Jon nodded. "I told her first."

Father arranged for Ramon to carry Jessie into the Convent Chapel that afternoon.

Mark Wilte, for the second day, devoted part of his column to the tender mercies shown by three patients to the petite nun who had passed away peaceably at her home during the night. Jon marveled how quickly the newsman had learned of Sister's home going.

Dr. Forbes ordered a complete physical for Father Jon, blood tests, x-rays and another stress test on the strength of his injured leg. "You're kidding," Jon responded when therapy informed him.

132

"No," Christy answered. "You are scheduled for fasting blood tests next Wednesday at eight in the morning, then x-ray at 2:30 the same day. The following day, we will do the stress test here at ten in the morning.

"Is he going to put me 'under' for the stress test?" Jon asked, remembering the scare they had the last time.

"I don't think so, but I can ask him if you would like."

Jon nodded as he got up from the exercise table with considerable ease. He no longer used a walker, and most of the time he went about without his cane.

He went upstairs to share the news with Jessie. "I guess I should have been expecting this," he told her. With the fund drive winding down and all."

"I know the drive has been very successful, Father." Jessie smiled. "I have heard good reports of much appreciation at having charts posted where staff and others were kept informed about the progress of the fund drive"

"The wrap-up banquet planning is well under way also," Jon smiled. "The results are better than we might have hoped for. Of course, we have had your professional planning and guidance."

"And Edith Von Himmel's leadership," Jessie added.

Later that afternoon, Father Jon hunted up Ramon. "Come see me after you're off," he told his friend.

Ramon looked at Jon with surprise. "Trouble somewhere?"

"No," Jon laughed, "Just a sneaking suspicion that my days here will soon end."

"A death threat?"

Jon laughed again, "More than likely a new assignment."

If Jon suspected that his days might be numbered at St. Elizabeth's Hospital, the blinking light on his phone increased his concerns greatly. He punched the answering device and listened to three different patients ask for his services. The fourth call arrested his thoughts as the Bishop requested a meeting for the next morning at the Bishop's office. "Well, Jon, it looks like it is sooner than even Dr. Forbes plans," he murmured aloud.

Jon made an effort to visit with patients that evening after eating in the cafeteria with some of the soon leaving interns. Ramon had found him in deep conversation with the interns so he promised to stop by in the morning. "Oh yes, I need a ride to the Bishop's office at eleven," Jon grinned at him. "Think you can manage that?"

Ramon laughed. "It'll be on my scheduled duties when I come in tomorrow morning, I am sure." Jon remembered the crisp morning nearly two years ago when he was called before the Bishop after Nadine died. A lot had happened in the intervening time, including the bullet in his leg. Jon carried his cane with him as a precaution, even though he could now climb steps and walk without assistance. It was a plain thing, his cane; all functional use and no show. Sort of like me, he thought as he waited in the tiny reception room like he had before. A stern-faced cleric announced that the Bishop would now see him.

"Father Jon, so glad you could make it on such short notice." The Bishop indicated one of the two chairs near the windows. "I like to look out at the birds and plants in my little private garden." Bishop James Paul laughed softly. "It," he pointed to the well kept twelve foot square just outside his windows, "is relaxing, and I am not responsible for it.

134

That in itself is enough to pull me to these windows often."

"I am fond of the Atrium at the hospital, especially in the early mornings when the caretakers are busy. It is relaxing to watch them restore the plants to their best." Jon hoped keeping the theme the Bishop had opened with was not out of order.

"Precisely," responded Bishop James Paul as he picked up a folder that was lying on the small table beside him. "I understand that Dr. Forbes has slated a series of tests to evaluate your recovery. And I imagine you are wondering if this meeting is to inform you of a new assignment."

"St. Ignatius again?" Jon dared to ask.The Bishop laughed. "No, you are going to remain at the hospital for a little while longer. I thought you came in a bit hesitantly." He flipped open the folder. "I have the preliminary totals for the fund drive. Remarkable work. If you hadn't grabbed at the gossip and given it direction, there is no telling what would have happened to the struggling finances of St. Elizabeth's."

Jon was looking at the predicted outcome totals for the fund drive. "You know, Edith Von Himmel, Jessica and the tenor, Philippe La Costa, all are part of this response as well as anything that I contributed. And Sister Margaret Louise," he added.

"I know, Jon, and I respect each of those whom you just named for their contribution to St. Elizabeth's Hospital. But, it has been your name that most associate with the drive."

"Cause I took a bullet in the leg," Jon stated.

"No, because you fought for what was right for the whole city."

Jon was studying the lack of shine on his shoes. How did I get here without noticing they needed polishing? he asked himself.

"Father Jon, are you listening to me?"
Jon's head jerked up as his face reddened. "I'm sorry, Your Excellency, I guess my mind wandered. Please forgive me."

"That is not exactly a sin, son. I was saying that I want you to restore the chapel at St. Elizabeth's so that the Eucharist can be celebrated there regularly. I want another room to be dedicated for public usage of any and all faiths for those who are reluctant to use the Catholic Chapel. There is sufficient money available to accomplish this task. The current acting administrator, soon to be promoted to full administrator, has already agreed to the plan and has another room set-aside for quiet meditation. Your job is to see that it all happens, along with your daily chaplain work."

The two men were now looking at each other. "What is the time schedule to accomplish this?" Jon looked down at the folder the Bishop handed him. "These look like architectural sketches."

"They are. As you can see, there is provision for a small conference room for counseling to be used by whomever has need." The Bishop flipped over several sheets of paper. "It is well thought out and privately funded by an anonymous donor. The Board of Directors has approved. Oh, by the way, the same Board asked that you implement the plans because of the respect the community has for you."

Jon's eyes shot to the Bishop's face. Now his face truly reddened. "I am not worthy of that compliment, Your Excellency. I am just a simple priest recovering from a misguided bullet injury and serving as a Chaplain to earn my keep."

"There is nothing simple about you, Jon." Bishop James Paul's use of his Christian first name in such a familiar tone touched deep within Father Jon's

136

spirit. "Everything you lay a hand on is affected in one way or another, and often in complex ways that can only be explained as God given."

The embarrassment that spread over Father Jon at his Bishop's personal statement left him feeling even more inadequate. "I don't understand," he murmured.

"There is nothing to understand. Just keep on doing as your heart leads you. The rest is up to the Father, the Son, and the Holy Spirit."

After a time of prayer, the two men parted. The Bishop, having heard Father Jon's confession, gave him absolution and his blessing. Jon carried with him the folder with details of the changes for the Chapel at St. Elizabeth's Hospital.

The celebration for the end of St. Elizabeth's Hospital fund drive began in the morning with an outdoor celebration of the Eucharist. It was held in a huge donated tent. A free carnival for all the children of the community was held at one of the city parks that afternoon. In the evening, a banquet was held in the tent for all who had participated in the fund drive. The reporters, local and national, swarmed the events, hoping to catch a glimpse of the famous trio who had precipitated the fund drive.

Father Jon assisted the Bishop at the Mass. Philippe, Jessie and Edith Von Himmel occupied a secluded area during the Eucharist, well surrounded by Hospital Security and Ramon. In the afternoon, there were sightings of Father Jon at the carnival, always protected from the press by Ramon and others. Jessie, in her wheelchair, led important visitors thorough public areas of the hospital narrating the future changes about to take place. The booming voice of Philippe La Costa could be heard telling about the wonders of the new enlarged atrium to be added on to the present atrium. The reporters were left to tag-a-long and see but never allowed access to the trio.

Early in the morning, Edith Von Himmel issued a written statement, with possible interviews after the banquet. The Bishop, and the new administrator, along with and St. Elizabeth's Board of Directors, received a check and pledge documentation.

"Bishop, what do you see as the reason for such a large turnout for this fund drive?"

The Bishop looked slightly amused. "If you attended the Eucharistic celebration this morning, you heard me give the credit. Just in case you missed that," and he smiled as though he had a big secret, "credit goes to the grace of God."

This was not the answer the reporters were looking for. "What about Father Jon's role?"

The Bishop turned and looked toward Father, who was standing near by. "Father?"

"God's grace."   Jon knew the reporters would not accept that answer readily.

"Father Jon," a new voice popped up.
"Didn't you think up this idea, and because of the notoriety of your previous injury, people just automatically follow you?"

"If that were so, hopefully they were following the 'Jesus' in me." Jon cast a quick glance at the Bishop for affirmation. An almost imperceptible nod by his Bishop encouraged him. "In reality," Jon continued, "I only acted upon the rumors that said I was going to 'save' the hospital. The rest was under the guidance of fellow patients, Jessie, and Philippe, and our volunteer Chairperson, Edith Von Himmel, and the hard work and many hours of the volunteers."

There was clamoring for more details that

138

Edith Von Himmel graciously answered. She reminded the reporters that she had made a detailed report available to them that morning, and most answers could be found in it.

The reporters turned to interview Philippe and Jessie, only to see the massive shoulders of the tenor as he pushed Jessie's wheelchair out the back of the tent. Several scurried after the two, to be met by Ramon and Hospital Security.

The whole hospital sighed with relief as normal activity became the rule of the day again. Philippe made plans to move into a nearby high rise apartment building. There was yet extensive plastic surgery to be complete on his wounds. He began practicing for a concert to be held later in the year with other well-known tenors. His wife withdrew her lawsuit under pressure from the attorneys, although she refused any reconciliation with Philippe.

Jon and Philippe were talking in Philippe's new apartment. "Magnificent view of the hospital," Jon laughed.

"Yes, I can watch the new construction on the atrium without getting up from my chair." Philippe's rumbling laugh followed. "You know, I have a better view of the changes than most people."

"Is that why you selected this apartment?"

"I chose this apartment because of the privacy features, and, of course, it is close to you and Miss Jessie."

"You can see the convent, too, and a glimpse of where Sister Margaret Louise is buried." Jon smiled as he remembered when that particular apartment building was first put up, and the offense the sisters at the convent expressed that their privacy within their gardens was invaded by whoever lived in the apartments.

As though Father had spoken his thoughts

aloud, Philippe spoke. "I understand the builder gave the convent a large donation to remedy that; higher walls, bigger trees and covered walkways. It is the first piece of gossip that pops up here when a new tenant moves in." He rubbed his large hands together. "I hope they don't get offended when I practice my singing with the windows open."

"If the songs are as beautiful as the one you sang to sister, I doubt they will object."

Philippe changed the topic, "How is the Chapel renovation coming along?"

"Slow. We have to do the extra room first. You would be amazed at those who try to block the opening of that second room. It seems that everyone had a plan for that 'orphan' room, and none of those plans had ever been expressed until the new administrator announced the renovations." Jon laughed. "I am putting out a lot of 'fires' as I attempt to see this project through."

"And praying, I would imagine," Philippe interjected.

Jon nodded.

After a pause, Philippe volunteered, "Jessie has been coming over to see me."

"To hear you sing?"

"That, and to have someplace to go that isn't hospital."

"Who brings her?" Jon asked.

"Usually an aide or Ramon."

"Do they stay while she is here?"

Philippe looked downward. "No, that is why I am telling you."

"You are concerned with the impropriety it might reflect on Jessie?"

Philippe nodded.

Jon sat back on his chair. "She brings you a lot of joy, doesn't she?"

Philippe nodded again.

"And you give her a lot of encouragement."

Another nod.

"Are you in love with her?"

Large tears rolled down Philippe's face. "As a dear child," he murmured. "I am an old man, a married old man."

"You never had any children, Philippe?"

"No," he whispered.

Jon knew what advice would normally be given in such a situation. "Jessie needs time away from the hospital, doesn't she? I remember the first outing I had. It was exhilarating."

Philippe nodded. "It gives her courage to face the next surgeries and that someday she will be independent again." Philippe mopped his face and blew his nose. "We became good friends during the fund drive. I didn't know I would miss her visits so when I moved over here."

Slipping to his knees, Jon bowed his head in prayer. "Will you join me in prayer, Philippe? Jesus is the answer."

Philippe and Jon spent some time in both spoken and unspoken prayer. A peace settled over the tenor as he hesitantly and tearfully gave up Jessie's visits. Father Jon rejoiced at the gentle leading of the Holy Spirit in Philippe.

Philippe La Costa called Jessie and told her of his decision to not have her come to his new apartment again. Gently, he explained his reasons, and they cried together over the telephone. He suggested that he visit her in the hospital and that he would take her places as she became able, but his apartment was now off limits to her. "I told Father Jon of my concerns," he said softly.

"Did he tell you that you could not have me over again?" Jessie's voice had hardness in it. This was something that Philippe had never heard before.

"No, little one. We prayed, and God told me."

"Oh," she whimpered. "Now, I am stuck here again forever!"

Her self-defeated voice sounded so much like his own bouts with depression that he almost cried. Then he thought of the question Jon had asked him about the children he never had.

"Jessie, I have to think and pray about this awhile before we talk again. I want you to do the same, think and pray. I know you pray and you hear God. Ask him for guidance." La Costa's voice was filled with a strength Jessie had never heard before. "I will be talking again with you in a few days. Lean on your God, Jessie. Goodbye, little one." The phone line went dead before Jessie could respond.

Jessie cried. When the nurses came in to help her from her wheelchair, they found Jessie with her head buried in her hands and an array of spent tissues on the floor.

"Are you in pain?"

Jessie shook her head as she allowed them to put her back to bed. She continued on with her broken sobs. Dr. Forbes ordered something for pain until he could get up to see her. She refused the medication.

Father Jon was eating with a group of new interns. He was surprised that the cynicism of the previous interns in their later months of internship was not in the hopefulness of this new group. Was that a product of internship, he wondered? He also noticed that most of this group had expressed a faith level that had been lacking in the last group. He rejoiced in this.

After the group disbanded, Jon sat on, lost in

his thoughts. "May I join you, Father?"

"Certainly, Melody. Melody? What are you still doing here? Didn't you complete your internship?"

Melody laughed. "Oh yes." But she did not say anything more.

"So why are you still here," he was looking straight at her.

"A special course in HIV/Aids children. I decided I wanted to add that to my certification. It is an intense three months on the latest medications and nutritional breakthroughs for children born with the HIV virus."

"Is it that prevalent in our country now? My goodness, I must really be out of touch." Jon was trying to catch up with this new development.

"Not here, yet, Father, but in the third and fourth world countries, it is the plight of many of the orphans."

"You almost sound like my cousin Leah. She works in an orphanage of HIV throw away babies."

Melody laughed. "You gave me her name and address last spring. We have been writing ever since."

"I did? Oh yes, I did, didn't I. Are you going to work someplace like that?"

Melody stifled her grin and giggle as Ramon entered the nearly empty cafeteria. "May I join you, Father?"

Jon looked at his buddy and nodded. "Do you know this former, or is it still, intern? Melody, this is Ramon, an old friend. Ramon, Melody, one of the saner interns of the past year."

The two looked at each other and acknowledged the introduction. Ramon sat down beside Melody. "Am I interrupting anything?" he asked.

Jon's thoughts were still tumbling over the confession of Philippe of the afternoon. No sin had been involved, but it certainly could have some negative ramifications for Jessie and Philippe, particularly if his wife learned of the innocent tryst. He was barely listening to Ramon and Melody.

"You know, I don't think he is listening to a word we are saying" Ramon commented.

Father Jon turned to look at these two friends of his and confessed that he had not been listening. "I am sorry. What did you say Ramon?"

Ramon grinned and said, "Friend, you are disturbed by something. Is there anything we can do to ease your mind?"

Melody struggled to not laugh aloud, for that was not what Ramon had said a moment before.

Jon shook his head. "I just was startled by a confession this afternoon, and obviously I haven't left it at the altar."

"Speaking of altar, Father, I am to make my first communion next Sunday. Could you be there?"

"First communion?" Jon echoed. His eyes were burrowing into Melody's. "Where? Who is the catechist?"

"Father Marvin at St. Ignatius. We, I did not think that it was wise to study under you in case the other interns thought you would try to convert them also."

"Father Marvin? How did you choose him?" "Ramon suggested him. He thought you would approve of the choice."

"I am delighted you have chosen to unite with the Catholic Church, Melody. It just comes as a total surprise. I am just awe struck."

If Father Jon had been looking at the two across from him, he would have realized there was more to the story. As it was, he was adjusting his personal schedule in his mind to be at St. Ignatius on Sunday. "Ramon, can you get me there on Sunday?"

'I have arranged for Scar to pick you up. He has his license now. He does the driving for St. Ignatius now that I am not there. Father Marvin would like you to concelebrate if you would."

Jon nodded. "I would be honored to."

"Father?" Melody paused. "When the Chapel is finished here, will you be able to have weddings in it?"

Something in Jon's spirit tensed. "I suppose so, although I would not expect that to be a normal function. The plan of the Bishop is to have a daily Eucharist celebration for those in the hospital that would desire it and communion available to those who are unable to come to the chapel. This is going to be a truly handicap-accessible chapel. In one of my first pastorates, we built a handicap ramp to the church as a special project, and the whole town benefited. You never can tell what might happen. Weddings, why not?"

"Has somebody asked you about that, Ramon?" Jon looked at his friend.

"No, but we were just wondering if you would marry us there in a few months?"

"Us?" Jon's voice echoed as his vocal chords tighten. His face paled, and his breathing became shallow. "You and Melody? Didn't I just introduce you?"

"No, friend. We have been courting for several months now."

Jon put his hands up to his face, as Philippe had, wanting both to laugh and cry at the same time. "This is a joke? A dream?"

"It is real, my friend," Ramon reached out and touched Jon. "Let us tell you the complete story."

145

They adjourned to a private corner of the atrium, where Jon heard the whole story. His pager went off once but he ignored it. "Let me get this straight. You two are going to the House of Hope, where my cousin is. You, Melody, are to be the doctor, and Ramon will be part of the team to minister to the HIV children. To God be the praise and glory! What an answer to prayer!"

Deep inside Father Jon's spirit, he felt the loss of his dear, strong friend while at the same time he rejoiced in the providence of God and the blessing Melody and Ramon would be in that mission. In Jon, the seed of longing to sometime go and serve among the poor and lowest grew a little bigger.

His pager vibrated with insistency.   Dr. Forbes was seeking him! Excusing himself from Ramon and Melody, who were glowing from their announcement, Jon hurried to a house phone.

"Jon, where have you been? I have been trying to reach you for over an hour. Jessie is in a deep depression. She is refusing my medical help. I have gotten her to agree to talk with you. Can you come now?"

Jon moved as fast as he dared without his cane to the nearest elevator. Dr. Forbes met him in the hallway. "Jessie won't tell us what she is crying about. The nurses say she has been like this since just before they put her back to bed late this afternoon."

"I may know what set her off," Jon replied grimly.   "You have not been able to get any medication into her?"

"No! She refused supper also. If she stays this way, this will precipitate a major setback in her physical healing. I would be reluctant to submit her to any more therapy or restorative surgery. She probably would refuse anyway."

"Let's pray before I go in there," Jon

146

suggested. A couple of the nurses stopped what they were doing to join the two men in prayer before Jon slipped into Jessie's room.

Jessie heard the door open and close but chose not to see who had come in. Jon sat down in a chair close to her bed and waited. Jessie tossed her legs, encased in special braces, back and forth on her bed as she moaned and sometimes sobbed. Occasionally, one of her brace-encased legs would collide with a bang against the metal rails of her bed, and her painful outcry caused her to momentarily stop her movements.

Jon prayed, beseeching the Lord for what to say to Jessie. After what seemed like a very long time, Jessie seemed to loose the rhythm of her moans and tossing. Still, Jon did not speak.

Dr. Forbes waited tensely. He almost wished he had not agreed to honor the priest's request that the intercom remain turned off. As the noise heard through the closed door lessened, the doctor's anxiety increased.

Finally, Jessie was still. Jon knew she hadn't fallen asleep, for she would inhale more sharply periodically as it was apparent that her legs were hurting her.

"You once asked me to be your advocate," Jon announced himself quietly. "Do you want one now?"

Jessie moaned, and Jon saw tears rolling down her face.

"It takes effort to ask for an advocate, Jessie, remember?"

She nodded her head slightly. She still had not opened her eyes to see him. Another pain passed up one of her legs, and she cried out briefly.

"Will you let Dr. Forbes help you with the pain?"

From between clenched teeth, Jessie said, "No!"

"Not ready yet to give up your anger, huh," Jon said softly. "Want to hurt more. OK." He sat back in the chair and waited, watching her face. He could see tears running down her face.

Jon began petitioning God audibly. Jessie cried out "Stop!" Jon ignored her request as he told God of Jessie's desire to hurt herself, of her anger with everyone including God, and lastly, of her relationship with Philippe. Several times she ordered him to cease his praying, but he did not.

Picking up a Bible from the nightstand, he began to read scripture to her. At first, she was restive. After he had been reading for ten minutes or so, she seemed to relax. There were no more sudden outcries of pain.

When he stopped suddenly in the middle of a passage, Jessie's eyes opened. Jon was looking straight at her. She closed them again. "You once asked for an advocate. Do you want one now?"

Jessie looked at him and nodded.

"His name is Jesus Christ."

She nodded, "I know," she said faintly.

"He is here, Jessie. Here and waiting. You have known him well over the years. He saved your life in the accident. He saved your legs. He has given you a good mind, Jessie. Use it for Him, not against him."

"I don't know how," she stuttered out softly.

"You have read this Bible and have scriptures marked that tell you how. Do you want me to read them to you?"

"No," she whispered.

"That is good, for it isn't that you don't know how, it is that you are refusing to admit you have taken sin back into your life." Jessie turned her face

148

away from Jon's penetrating look. "That is true, isn't it?"

Jessie nodded.

"I do not have to know your sins, Jessie. You do not have to confess them aloud to me, but you do have to bring them before God and ask for forgiveness. Do you want me to leave the room while you do that?"

"No," she blurted out, "Stay."

For a while, neither spoke. Jessie rehearsed in her mind how she had offended God until the silence was unbearable.

"Help me start," she whispered.

Jon did.

The doctor looked up from his own meditations when Jon came out of Jessie's room. "She will accept help from you now." Jon walked slowly to the elevator. He was relieved when it opened as soon as he had gotten there. The secrecy of confession was valid for any Christian.

The orphan room, once freed from it several other job descriptions, for which one person or another had assigned it, became a tastefully appointed room. Various religious themes were developed in separate corners of the room. The first week it was opened, the comments received were gratifying. A small attached room became an intimate room for those who were grieving or needed quiet counsel.

The new administrator called Father Jon into his office. "It looks like the new 'Quiet Room', as they named it, is going to be a hit."

Father Jon nodded. "Now to the Chapel."

"Yes, I talked with the Bishop just yesterday to get him to release the rest of the funds for the renovation of the Chapel. I have the name of the contractor who has agreed to do the work." He handed a piece of paper to Father Jon.

"Do I need to contact him?" Jon asked.

"The Bishop did. I got a phone call from the man early this morning. He will be here this afternoon to look over the Chapel and plan the work. The Bishop said you would be in charge of this phase."

Jon acquiesced. "The plan is to have it closed on only a limited basis while this work is going on."

"I concur," the Administrator said. "It will be a blessing to have the availability of the Eucharist and Mass in the hospital proper. We are like a compact, specialized city. Will you be the priest assigned here to serve daily Mass, Father?"

A little chuckle escaped Father's throat.

"The Bishop hasn't said. Dr. Forbes has pretty much given me a clean bill of health this past week. Possibly the Bishop will have another assignment for me as an able-bodied priest."

"It has been a real advantage having 'our own' priest here," the Administrator affirmed. "If the Bishop does move you, which is his prerogative, I feel certain it will be for a good cause."

"All the money being invested in the new Chapel and the Quiet Room indicates a deep interest by the Bishop to maintain the spiritual-side of this hospital. I feel certain he will not leave this work understaffed. Didn't you tell me last week three of the current other Chaplains have been asked to oversee the Quiet Room?" Father Jon asked.

"Two, the third one is to be a Catholic priest, from the instructions the Bishop has shared with me. I was just curious if you were to be that man?"

Jon laughed. "If I am, I don't know it yet."

"I guessed that from our conversation this morning. I suppose I was sort of prying, wasn't I?"

150

A small smile played on the Administrator's lips. "Sorry, Father, it was juvenile of me. Please forgive me."

"As the Admin, you don't like secrets or surprises, if you can help it," Jon answered back. "No sin in that, Leroy, just curiosity."

As he waited for the assigned contractor that afternoon, Jon thought over the morning's conversation. Well, Jon, if what the Admin said is true. . . His thoughts rambled around as he attempted to remember something the Bishop had said at the end of the fund drive. Finally, he murmured to himself softly, "We'll see."

The contractor was an older man. "I have been briefed by the Bishop," the contractor said abruptly as he shook Father's hand. The new seats and carpet are already in the warehouse. I am to make certain the room will last as long as the hospital. I am to refurbish the actual platform the altar sits on according to architectural drawings already done. You do have a copy of them, Father?" The man paused and looked Jon in the eye.

"Right here," Jon pointed to where he had laid them on the bare floor.

"Good," the contractor smiled slightly. "We are on the same page. Bishop James Paul said you had a copy. I appreciate that you have stripped the room of all unnecessary objects. That speeds up my work."

"Have you ever worked on a Catholic Chapel or Church?" Jon parried.

The man nodded. "I know the do's and don'ts regarding attention to religious objects. I just finished the restoration of the part of the Cathedral that was bombed and burned by that madman."

"Then you know who I am?" Jon peered into the contractor's eyes.

"Yes, you took the bullet," the older man said sensitively. "You risked your life and won, bless the name of the Lord."

"Yes, the Lord is responsible for the halting of that 'madman' as you called him and preserving my life. I owe everything to God, the Father; His son, Jesus; and the Holy Spirit," Jon said humbly.

The work began in earnest that day, and within forty-five days, the chapel was ready for dedication. It was to be a solemn ceremony, with the Bishop presiding and Father Jon concelebrating. Closed circuit television made the dedication Mass available to any and everyone who wished to participate within the hospital. Several large screen televisions were placed in the Atrium for those invited guests who wanted to watch and participate in the dedication Mass. Several priests assisted in the distribution of the Eucharist at various locations in the hospital.

After the dedication celebration that included tours of the new Chapel and a reception in the Atrium, the Bishop looked his faithful priest in the eyes and quietly said, "Your work here is finished, Father Jon."

Jon's heart skipped a beat before he responded. "Thank you."

"Be at the Chancery in the morning at ten."

"I will."

Back in his small apartment, Jon took inventory of his feelings. He was not surprised. There had been many clues over the past few months, and he knew he was ready to leave the chaplaincy. However, it hurt to think of saying goodbye to all of his friends in the hospital. He dropped to his knees with thanksgiving that he could once again kneel or even lie prone on the floor to pray.

Father Jon couldn't sleep. He packed his

meager belongings and about midnight began to walk the quiet halls of the hospital, stopping in the 'premie' nursery, the cancer wing, the ER, and elsewhere to pray with staff or patients who were having a tough night. He would miss all of this, including the sudden jolt when ER called him in the middle of the night. He was amazed to discover how all that went on within the big hospital seemed normal to him, even though the hospital's work involved abnormal illness, injuries, death and grief.

Shortly before sunrise, he returned to his quarters to shower and catch a nap. He left a call for Ramon to take him to the Chancery. He had no doubt that Ramon had it on his schedule when he came to work that day. Briefly, he wondered what the Bishop would do when Ramon married, and he and his wife left for the children's home overseas.

The phone awoke him, ringing at his elbow. For a moment, he forgot his appointment as he automatically reached for the instrument. "Father Jon," he spoke into the receiver.

Ramon's voice returned to him. "Just making sure you are ready to go, Jon. I will pick you up in the front circle, O.K.?"

"How soon?" Jon glanced at his watch.

"Ten minutes." The line went silent.
After a quick, last minute glance in the mirror, Father ambled toward the lobby. It was just beginning to get busy there. He nodded at the main receptionist as he went by the desk. "I will be out for the rest of the morning," he told the girl who did the paging. She nodded.

"Have a nice time," she responded with a smile. She put 'out' by his name on the chart she kept.

Ramon stood ready by the car as Father Jon carefully climbed in. This movement was still a little tricky for Jon in the passenger seat, with nothing to hold on to like the steering wheel on the driver's side.

"We are going to the Chancery, right?" Ramon glanced at Father Jon's placid face.

"Yes, may be a one way trip."

Ramon kept silent. He was aware that Father was probably going to be moved to a new assignment. They had spent several evenings talking about it in the last couple of weeks.

"My things are all packed and sitting in my rooms. You won't have any difficulty in retrieving them for me, will you?"

"You don't plan to go back to say goodbye?" Ramon was surprised.

"No, I did that my way last night. Too many people would want to see me and say too many things." Jon sighed softly. "I am ready to leave for a new place." His voice seemed to quiver.

"Does Jessie know?"

"I'll phone her and have a long talk after I know where I am going."

"That will be hard on her." Ramon turned into the long drive to the Chancery.

She is a big girl. She'll manage. Philippe will be keeping in touch with her. That will help her. You could go by and see her," Jon turned with a half smile towards his friend.

Jon walked up to the door and knocked. It was opened as it always was by the granite-faced priest. He was ushered into the small waiting room with the explanation that the Bishop would see him in a few minutes. Some things never change, Father Jon thought as he sat on the dreadfully straight chair to wait. As stealthily as a thief, the granite-faced priest disappeared through another door. Jon made a wry face as he briefly remembered other times in that waiting room.

154

The door to the Bishop's office opened with a sharp click. "Come in, Father Jon." The Bishop stood in the doorway smiling at the priest. "Did you eat breakfast this morning?"

"No, you Excellency."

"I thought maybe not." The Bishop smiled, "I have sent for a late breakfast to be served in a few minutes. You will partake with me?" Jon took a seat at the small table in front of the windows as the Bishop indicated. "You didn't sleep much last night either."

Father Jon looked up abruptly at his Bishop. "Who told you?"

The Bishop chuckled and pointed upward before he said, "I know you."

After they ate and chatted awhile, Bishop James Paul moved toward his desk. "I suppose we need to transact business now." He picked up a thick manila folder. With a clatter, car keys slid out onto the otherwise immaculate desk. "Your new assignment, Father Jon, is to assist the current pastor at Our Lady of Perpetual Peace.

Assist? Jon thought. He fixed his eyes on his Bishop.

"No comment?" The Bishop asked.

"I am waiting for 'the rest of the story' as a famous radio commentator used to say."

"Father Ott is past retirement age. He has refused retirement and/or replacement for a number of years. I suspect his health is questionable. I sent a couple of envoys, undercover, of course, to try to get a good picture of what is going on."

Jon nodded his head as the Bishop continued.

"What they found was a very gentle man, nurturing 'his' special project, the shrine or grotto-like church that has been creating a legend in his time. He is fearful that the diocese will just shut it down or take away from what his vision is. I have asked advice of several different 'orders' that are caretakers for similar popular tourist haunts."

"And they aren't interested in Father Ott's church/shrine?" Jon asked. Father Ott was a legend even before he had gone into the priestly life. "Aren't there claims of the miraculous taking place up there?"

"I thought you might have heard of them. So far, they are only stories. No one has submitted any documentation." The Bishop smiled. "Mostly they seem to be stories of exceptional peace."

"Back to my investigative envoys," the Bishop continued after glancing at the documents in the folder in his hands. "You know one of them."

It was Jon's turn to smile, "Ramon, I suppose."

"Yes."

"Did he suggest that I might be the 'perfect' priest to go up there?" There was a twinkle in Father Jon's eyes.

"No, but I won't be surprised that he suspects I will be sending you there." The Bishop's face grew solemn. "It is time Father Ott retires. He has worked tirelessly almost all of his life as a priest in that work. The previous Bishop just ignored him, so I inherited a stubborn and tenacious priest who serves faithfully. He answers all my inquires respectfully and always encloses a large donation above the normal for the diocese as Our Lady of Perpetual Peace has many supporters."

"But to willingly retire, he won't?" Father Jon asked.

"No, he is so afraid we will bulldoze down his work."

"Doesn't he consider it God's work?"

"He has until very recently. I find some

156

confusion in his answers to my letters now. He met with the Chancellor last month at my request."

The Bishop strolled over to his 'private garden' windows. "You know, I have a number of different kinds of birds to come to my feeders out there. There are the aggressive crows, the numerous pigeons and/or doves, the common sparrows, blue jays, cardinals and a couple of robins that winter over. Nevertheless, they are all birds. Occasionally, even a group of finches fly in for a free meal."

Jon's eyes followed to where the Bishop was looking. A couple of sparrows were arguing over the same spot on the feeder. He knew without any word being spoken that the Bishop was pointing out the many different priests under the Bishop's care. And how different each one was, even to scrapping over the same territory.

"I never get an eagle out there." The Bishop looked back at Jon. He returned to his desk.

"The Chancellor asked Father Ott to accept an injured priest who still needs time to rest and acclimate back into regular priestly duties. Of course, Father brought up the lack of room in his 'cottage', yes that is what he calls it, to accommodate another priest. Then, after some thought, he decided that the two small rooms upstairs could be readied for you."
"Does he know who I am?"

"A humble priest in need of some peace." The Bishop said slyly.

Father Jon thought a moment. "What am I to do there?"

"Rest, and . . ."

"And?" Jon saw a smile playing around Bishop James Paul's face.

"Gently take the burden off Father Ott. I sense he will be leaving us soon."

"Information gathered by the envoys?"

There was only a slight nod of the Bishop's head. They talked for some time about Father Jon's role at Our Lady of Perpetual Peace. "I took the liberty of exchanging your car for one more suited for the high country you are going into. This one has all wheel drive. I don't want you hindered in your travels in the area. Some of the parishioners live back in the hollers and the coves, barely accessible."

Jon, following the directions of the granite-faced priest, found the new all-wheel drive SUV sitting in the parking lot of the Chancery. Inside it were all of his belongings from St. Elizabeth's, along with a note and a mysterious package from Ramon.

> *Dear Friend,*
> *I took the liberty to pick up your*
>
> *things at the hospital since you were*
>
> *so long with our Bishop. Don't open*
>
> *the package until you get to your new*
>
> *home.*
>
> *Your friend, Ramon*

A road map with the directions to Our Lady of Perpetual Peace was on the passenger seat. Jon sat and cried. He was surprised that his emotions were so tenderly influenced by the love shown him by the Bishop and Ramon.

158

Herman Ott stared at the letter. The young priest was arriving today! He wasn't ready yet. The rooms upstairs were ready, thanks to a couple of parishioners who cheerfully helped Father remove the years of collections he had stored there. A new storage building sat twenty feet back from the 'cottage' with those things he was reluctant to discard. He had not intended to expose his heart feelings to others, but these men seemed to understand about his keepsakes.

Herman shuffled slowly from the cottage over to the church. He needed peace in his heart for this gigantic undertaking. He fought many battles to bring about Our Lady of Perpetual Peace parish in the past. This battle, to let another man into this very private part of himself, was more frightening than any of the battles of the past. Tears ran down his face as he knelt before the altar.

It was there, at the altar, Father Jon found him, a tired old man, resting in the peace. "Father, I have come to share in your burden," Jon said as he knelt beside the frail man.

Father Herman looked at the young man beside him and said, "It is God's will."

From "Our Lady of Perpetual Peace", the next in the *Adventures of Father Jon Mark*

Penelope and her husband live near the Blue Ridge Parkway in northwestern North Carolina They share their home with a large herding dog, Maria. As a writer, Penelope has incorporated many places, people, animals and experiences of her life in her stories. Often a dog of character shows up in a story. There have been many dogs and other animals in her life. She taught math in high schools and colleges until she and her husband retired to the beautiful mountains to write full time.

Several years ago Penelope would have lost her eyesight had God not miraculously intervened. As an artist, a photographer, and a writer, she crafts her stories and art so they show the love of God for mankind.